T0300656

The Enhancers

Anne K. Yoder

meekling press 2022

Meekling Press
Chicago, IL
meeklingpress.com

Printed in the USA.

Cover art by Suzanne Gold

ISBN 978-1-950987-25-2

Library of Congress Control Number: 2022939009

For C.B., E.S., and my many other
abettors in escape.

O science! Everything's been taken care of. For the body and soul—the last rites—there's medicine and there's philosophy—old wives' remedies and new arrangements of popular songs. And the pastimes of princes and the games they've outlawed! Geography, cosmography, mechanics, chemistry... !

Science, the new nobility! Progress. The world moves ahead! Why shouldn't it turn?

Arthur Rimbaud, *A Season in Hell*

VALEDICTORIAN is available in 2.5mg tablets, 5mg capsules (pink /white), 10mg capsules (daisy/tangerine), 18mg XR capsules (gold/navy), and 28mg XR capsules (magenta/black).

I. INDICATIONS and USAGE

Some years flow smoothly. Others come crashing down. The year I started VALEDICTORIAN was the latter for me and my friends in Lumena Hills. V. was the latest supplement, the fifth-generation refinement of the "most advanced" chemical used to enhance and augment our memories. I'll admit I felt a small thrill knowing my brain would expand and that soon I'd be so smart, like a genius, even, but beyond that. VALEDICTORIAN boosted minds during our sharpest years. Carried forward, V. would make my generation so much smarter than any humans before. Or that's what we were told.

V. was a game changer. There had been "casualties" with earlier iterations, minds that couldn't handle the weight of information, minds that had caved in on themselves. That's why there were strict guidelines for administration and multiple antidotes. That's why we were told not to deviate from our regimens. That's why we spent so much time performing mental exercises, like memorizing Pi to its 100th decimal place, then its 1000th, then reciting. Not unlike playing scales on a piano. More advanced students then used Pi to compare and describe other circular items, like the shape of a pie, or the roundness of a face. This became a language unto itself.

We also had a language for the shape of a mind. We were told to envision that our minds on V. resembled one of a variety of fruit shapes. These shapes formed the foundations for storing information. Pineapple minds were the strongest and most articulated. We were encouraged to envision their neurons interlinked like solid diamonds and that these diamonds supported the aggregation of facts. Minds were also shaped like pomegranates. Pomegranate minds were more common, with ideas packed together side by side then sealed off, like apartment tenants, like networked computers. The shapes of lesser minds were less distinct. Think apples. Think avocados. Think minds without V. Problems arose when these minds encountered too much stress. Sometimes they were hollow. Sometimes the wrong regimen would rot their core.

And yet. We were often reminded how lucky we were to have this new tool. My parents Judy and Harold told me to imagine their lives before supplements. As if this were tragic. As if I could imagine anything but using chemical enhancements to think and feel and grow.

By the time I started taking VALEDICTORIAN I'd had plenty of practice. I'd taken test doses. I'd had multiple mind maps made and electronic monitoring of my brain waves. I knew that V. was about building a better future. That brain fall was a thing that had happened long ago. Its history, a whisper that I saw hints of in the blank faces of people who wandered Lumena's outskirts. Or maybe I imagined this. If I adhered to directions, took the terms of use seriously, I would not have problems.

I started taking V. in late summer along with the rest of my classmates entering third year. This gave us time to acclimate before classes started. I had known that starting V. would happen in this way seemingly forever. But no one had hinted that taking a full regimen would feel quite so grim.

In the last weeks of summer, smoke from the factory's stacks fell low in the morning like a fog. The smoke swept between our houses and through the streets in the valley below. We were told to stay inside but I didn't need instructions to do this. I always spent mornings in the basement. I heard the hum of the air filter running on high as I toggled between screens and moved animals between lists—from endangered to extinct. I'd made a habit of tracking endangered species and their dwindling numbers. My friends Azzie and Celia assisted me with this. When numbers continued downward, I took note. This is what happened most of the time. Today it was announced that the last tufted puffin had died, mateless and in captivity. I felt a new sadness as I streamed video clips of the birds rubbing beaks. This puffin had great sideburns like mutton chops, that puffed out and made it look wise and wild like a cross between a professor and an old rocker. It was so hard for me to fathom how this bird roamed the earth for centuries and disappeared just like that.

"Species monitoring and maintenance" was how I listed this activity in my habit log for the morning, a log that I was required to keep as part of my own monitoring. This is what I was doing when Judy entered the room holding a hot-pink-and-white box. I looked up and then back to my spreadsheet.

"Hannah!"

"Umhhhm..."

"Didn't you hear the door?"

I looked over again. Judy was all sharpness, angled chin and knees poking out from her skirt. She dangled a box with the words StarterPAC in bold in front of me. She set the box down, pulled its contents out, then spread them on the table before us: four foil packs holding rows of electric-pink-&-white caps and promotional pins (as if I'd be caught dead wearing any of them).

Judy wanted me to start *now*. She told me to scan the code. Beside it in bold it said, READ BEFORE USE. And in smaller type: All users must be preapproved. *How obvi*, I thought but did not say. I knew the drill. All my friends had started or were about to, and we all talked and shared tips. But Judy wanted to do it by the book. Liability, blah blah blah, she said. The link took me to a video detailing the "full V. experience" which was narrated by Lumena's own Dr. Billy, bunco in charge of dosing and augmentation at school. Billy was known for his long, boring and all too frequent talks and his general enthusiasm for supplements. He had a pill, or many, for every condition. The video ended with testimony from alumni who'd gone on to achieve success, as the factory defined it—high-level positions with room for advancement.

I downloaded an app that featured a journal where I was supposed to track doses and record my experiences, both emotional and physical (together they were called "foundational"). I was required to do this for the next three weeks.

The first page asked me to begin with an audio clip, to articulate what I wanted to do with the BrainBoost™ that VALEDICTORIAN was about to introduce. As if it were my choice. I was asked to list three things I wanted to master and to imagine who I would become in a year, in five years, and over a lifetime. *Basic as fuck*, is what I thought. It's also what I said. Judy said to watch my mouth, and that the accuracy of my prediction wasn't the point, at least not right now.

I responded again. This time I said I wanted to become aware of the dying animals and rehabilitate their habitats. I said I wanted to save them. That one day I'd even go out to the savanna to live with them. This wasn't untrue though I knew it wasn't likely. I could tell Judy was frowning even though she was standing behind me. She didn't like death as a subject, or rewilding as a proposition, or my talking about either. She especially didn't like what she called my "preoccupation" with extinction. She said "just keep living" was the plan. That we should agree on that. I did. But that was also the reason I couldn't focus on anything but the ways this was not happening—with so many lifeforms endangered and dying it seemed like hubris to think that sooner or later this wouldn't also implicate us.

Some people said that V.'s first doses felt like a small jolt; others said they had electricity running through their bodies; some experienced pain and a paralysis of sorts. I wasn't scared despite knowing this. I just wondered what it would feel like to ingest, to experience. Mostly I wondered who I was about to become.

I laid the capsule on my tongue and swallowed. Then we sat. I felt nothing at first but then I felt everything at once. A rush overcame my body and I couldn't move. Judy started saying things and whatever she said, however her mouth moved, it sounded like squawk. She got up and ran to the next room and came back with an oversized purse. She placed her arms around me then pulled a thin syringe from the purse and placed its needle in my arm. A few moments later I began to feel loose. Judy helped me up the stairs and to bed. She lay beside me for a while, maybe the entire night. She was there the next morning when I came to. And then we started the same routine again.

During those first weeks of ACCLIMATION, I felt dizzy-headed most of the time. I couldn't think what to do in the morning, how to dress, or how to get out of bed. Judy and Harold intervened every so often with their assessments and uploads, monitoring my activities—could I walk? without pause?—and testing my memory: capacity, alacrity, uptake. I performed miserably. They set plates of food on trays in front of me but I was never hungry. I spent days in bed and if I made it out, then it was just hours on the couch.

It felt like I lived with something membranous between me and the rest of the world—the screen was the only thing. It was a portal to the animals, their video feeds, to film clips, to the whole fucking archive of utterances and ideas in the massive repository of the internet. I just sat and took it all in 24/7 as our cats Ismelda and Esmerelda stretched upon me and nuzzled my legs.

The first effects were the loudest. I remember that. The barrage of facts. A newfound awareness of our habitat's desperate circumstance. I had no interest in so much of what I was forced to absorb: the force of gravity, how to determine true north, mating habits of salmon swimming upstream. Most information quickly found its own space but the unwanted earworms often got out of hand—I had no way to say begone! skit! scatter! All of this information stuck like gold powder spilled into the crevices of my gray matter. Soon I learned I was an overreactor, easily stimulated and overly so. From the first my skin felt taut, my body stiff. I would sit for hours absorbing while holding in piss. Sometimes I stayed on task, other times I'd wander and watch packs of jaguars, their lithe bodies like bullets crossing the screen. I absorbed the vocabulary of twelve languages I didn't yet speak.

V. caught everything. My mind became a Venus flytrap. Suddenly I somehow knew the acidity of the ocean and, at our current rate of warming, how soon it would become inhospitable to life. The clutter in my head followed me everywhere too, manifesting physically in my bedroom where everything was strewn. My tabletops were filled with vials and powders and Harold's old film canisters I'd taken from his collection of antiquities, aka his crates in the basement. They were filled with so many old, dated objects: papers and animal pelts and petrified shark's teeth. Paper maps, globes, textbooks for physics and mathematics, and metal tools to make hand-drawn graphs. I loved to run my hands over these objects and their varied textures. I loved to look at images and their negatives—how funny to think of these films, as if they depicted an absence.

There was also this one live stream of chimpanzees I'd watch on the regular. I liked to peer through the leaves and branches as the chimps passed, circled back, and patted each other's asses—as if they knew their dramas played out before me. Sometimes but not often they'd do this aerialist thing I can't quite explain: they'd use their arms and feet to spin in the air and catch themselves using an intricate network of branches. And you know what? I never saw them sleep and I never saw them fuck. Though I did see the cousin yank himself off, after eating, only once. The jizz flew like a fount and was unlike anything I'd ever seen.

My favorite things about the chimps was what they did not do: stare at screens, put on white coats or any clothes at all, or act self-righteous AF. They didn't take supplements, didn't make flow charts, didn't track happiness scores. They touched each other's faces. They grabbed each other's arms and asses and wrestled in the mud. I wondered, if I could find them IRL, would they take me in?

Judy insisted that no one wondered such things. Beyond town, she'd told me, there were rusted out bridges, crumbling roadways, carapaces of old buildings. The towns between factory centers had fallen away, and between them the emptiness was filled with trees and terrain. Only a few people still lived out there, though the way Judy put it, they were dangerous or ignorant, and often both. "Just what are they hiding from," she'd say. I'd just shrug her off and accuse her of being so anthro. She had so many judgments about people, but she also needed to captivate them in her own way. She didn't care about the puffin or the chimps. But their lives didn't appear empty or unworthy to me. Living beyond town and closer to other lifeforms had always sounded kind of wild.

II.

School was a blur when classes started. I barely recall the contours of the days. They seemed to be filled with only my travels from home to school, often via the dispensary. I took doses it felt like every five minutes: every morning, at noon, later in the afternoon, with dinner, and before bed. Sometimes Judy would wake me in the middle of the night to swallow more pills. Of these days I recall the colors, mostly: the neon orange pill glowing in the dispensary window, the white box where I'd type in my number, the whoosh of the machine, and the clear plastic bins holding what seemed like millions of capsules, the white-and-blues, orange-and-reds, beige-and-blands. I'd spend the rest of the day adrift in a haze. When I think back to the time passing, all I conjure are streaks of color and light, and every so often, a face.

Toward the end of that first week, I began to move through days more distinctly. It felt odd to be swimming in so many facts and ideas that it was hard to keep track of the details of my days. Thursday afternoon, as soon as Power, Politics, and Leadership was dismissed, Azzie and Celia came over to me.

"You still up for the ceremony?" Azzie asked.

I looked up, confused. Azzie's blue curls almost

glowed in the light.

"We talked about it last night." Celia said.

I nodded, I thought, but I'm not sure why.

Azzie acted like I hadn't moved. She placed her hand on my forehead. I felt her hair against my cheek.

"Still breathing," she reported. "Hannah, you are not acting right."

"I know, I know."

"Look here." She queued her device, scrolled through a series of messages I recalled sending and receiving, like sometime last week. But here they were, timestamped yesterday: messages of the tufted puffin's demise and plans to hold an extinction ceremony after class today.

I was usually the one who led these ceremonies. We'd been doing them since first year, after I'd learned that so many animal lives and lineages were dying off. Azzie participated in the ceremonies to humor me, I think, and plus she always liked to be doing things. And Celia, she talked of the soul of the animals as the lifeline of our planet. The soul part didn't make much sense to me though I figured it was the influence of her mother's new age spirituality. But in some way it did, because I cared about them too. I wouldn't use those words, though. I didn't know what to call the feeling. Since starting V. I'd become overwhelmed. I'd developed a new awareness of death's magnitude. It didn't seem right to be ok with knowing this, and that we humans had been the ones to set it in motion. And yet most people kept right on with their lives. I didn't understand how they managed to do this.

Celia sat down in the seat beside me, took the antler pendant that hung from her neck. Her blonde hair was swept back in a loose braid, her dark roots showing. She twisted the antler from its base, then handed it to me. Her blood red nails held up the vial, its white powder within. It felt like some kind of consecration. I held the antler to my nose and inhaled. I held my breath and counted to three, and soon I felt tingly and relieved.

Azzie said she could lead today's ceremony. But that she wasn't taking no for an answer. I nodded and said, fine, if she insisted.

"Are you really this TMI?" she asked

Too Much Information was a state many of us fell into when starting V. Like oversharing, it offended the senses, so that daily activities took on a pallor. The dreariness of the everyday exceeded itself.

"YES," I said. About this I felt strongly.

Celia took her antler back from me, held it to her nose and inhaled. Her eyes narrowed and she began to breathe deeply. She shrugged. "Same with me, Hannah. Though a bump of D. always helps me."

Her doses of V., like mine, were taking longer to figure out. She'd had to cut her doses in half right away, then completely, and had to restart slowly. Her mother monitored her dosing times closely and made her come home on the regular to observe. On the continuum of information consumption and V., I was closer to Celia. Overwhelmed.

We took the path behind the school down to the river, then climbed the cement barriers and scrambled down to the rocky bank. Celia had brought a black cape that she spread over the rocks. She pulled out 3D miniatures of each animal that she'd printed with resin—a small tufted puffin, a bobcat, and a sociable weaver sparrow—and she placed them on the cape. Azzie set out a burner she'd swiped from the lab. She lit it, placed a small metal rack over it, then placed the bobcat on the rack. The figure started to smoke and burn. I documented each of these actions on my device. We followed with the sparrow, then the puffin.

Celia insisted we each pick a phrase and repeat it. *A mantra*, she called it. Celia was immersed in spiritual practices because of her mother who kept a Buddha in the backyard and who used a vat of holy water to clean her screens. The only reason no one shamed her mother more for her beliefs was that she was married to one of the most rational scientists at the factory.

When it came to a mantra, I had no practice. I didn't know what to say, so I muttered to myself, *You are free, fly away.* The entire process lasted about fifteen minutes. Azzie then streamed video clips of bobcats, sparrows, and puffins going about their lives. It was past tense, obvi, but in that moment it seemed as if they were still here.

The sun was going down by the time this ended. Azzie suggested we get on with tossing the ash. We climbed up on the rocks that stood between us and the river and threw the ash down, watching as the wind swept it away. This felt solemn, holy even—Celia said we were offering up their animal essences, as if we were on the Ganges. The factory was just beyond us, standing tall on the hill. Its smokestacks were monoliths, thick and white, and from them spun plumes. Today the smoke turned clear.

We then sat on the bank. Celia took her antler and passed it around. She soon lay back on a blanket and started talking dreamily about Samsun, how he was coming by her house later to help explain theories of spectroscopy and to prepare for a quiz on crystallography. "He says that natural light contains a rainbow," she cooed. "And that each atom has its own unique spectra—like a fingerprint. Isn't that delicious?"

I thought the only thing you two studied was anatomy," Azzie quipped.

Celia said, "Oh that too. I can tell you about the curvature of his specimen, and its output. He's virile."

"Please, no. That's vile." I didn't want to think about Samsun naked or in ecstatic mergence with my friend.

Celia's mind had its own spectra, leaning more to her mother's spirituality, and unwilling to absorb basic principles of the hard sciences. But she had more capacity than Samsun. This was obvious to me.

"He's low-bit, Celia. I don't get what you see."

"*You* wouldn't Hannah." They thought I was priggish. This was no secret.

"Look, I have no appetite for his frequency."

"For anyone's frequency." Azzie ribbed me.

"Not even my own of late, apparently."

Azzie asked what it felt like, my taking V.

"Sometimes I can't match my thoughts with my body," I said. "Though also, and only once, I felt lit—like incandescent."

She shook her head like she pitied me. When I asked what taking V. was like for her, she said, "Pure energy."

If this was true, I was jealous. I wondered what was so different within us that we would take the same chemical and experience it in opposite ways. I asked what she thought, and she said, "Your problem is you get tangled."

This was true, I supposed, but I didn't know what there was to do about it.

Celia's device vibrated.

"Lover boy," Azzie cooed.

Celia looked at her device, then shoved it in her bag. "My mom," she sighed. "She's all 'Pill time!

Come home.'" Celia's eyes narrowed and she opened her mouth as if she were about to hiss. She twirled her gold antler, then took one last dip. I did the same. She stumbled over her feet. I took her arm, and something about the pressure of her arm around my neck, or maybe the weight of her against me, it made me feel present, like I'd stopped drifting for a moment. Whatever it was, I felt grounded somehow, like for once I inhabited my body.

SOPORIFIC enhances frontal cortex activity, the primary source of cognition and creativity. Click here for data about the cost / benefit ratio.

That weekend the factory smoke blew up and we could go out. Its two smokestacks stood so tall on the hill, they could be seen from most perspectives. Smoke made little difference now to my staying in or going out, but I loved to see the stacks standing high in the sun like monuments. They were built the year our town, Lumena Hills, was established. Before then it had been a nowhere town, out of the way. Back then the town had been called Between. It had been a town falling into itself, and its history was divided into before and after the factory. At the time the town had been fading, with an aging astrophysics lab and a series of decrepit schools that prepared students for decrepit desk jobs they would gradually move through too. So much was different now with the boost that had begun with the factory.

Lumena Corp. was established in 1981. It was founded at the crest of the hill, with a river flanking each side. First came the factory, and then came the stream of postdocs in R&D. Some of the most forward thinkers in supplemental chemistry moved to this town which soon became a center for research and development and archival advances. This is where VALEDICTORIAN's predecessors were first conceived of and created. Lumena became one of many hubs spread out like nodules, each with its own specialty. Ours specialized in analyzing natural substances and developing biosimilar synthetics. These were called 'natural' products. The labs also produced thousands of new chemical structures each year. They were cataloged and stored for future use, reference, and retrieval in a series of chambers dug deep into the hill.

The town itself had developed an obsession with information. With information came dealing in acquisition and storage. This was a good thing, residents said. Easy to keep. Information fell through the air invisibly, coating our bodies. It flowed through the air like voices. There were true facts and fictional facts and false facts too, and no one disputed which fact belonged in which category.

Sometimes information in the air was so dense it accumulated in drifts. I'd seen people wander with vacant stares and suddenly come to. This seemed absurd to me before I started V. But now I stumbled into this too. It felt like entering a storm. Judy called these fits of losing my senses and stumbling about "increased turbulence." I could sense a heaviness in the air when it was full—some of us were more sensitive to its presence. Judy said it was possibly like a sixth sense we hadn't realized we possessed until we were burdened by the excess.

How much information could one memory hold? The question was often asked. It was rhetorical but was wielded to remind us: not much, on its own. The general theories of cognition suggested that a memory would expand to accommodate the volume of information ingested. Facts were dense, and too many would tear through.

ReMember [as in take three with a morning meal] remedies that.

The smoke blew downwind soon enough again. It descended and covered the town in a blanket of chemical sweetness. The days passed candy-coated, all surfaces were lickably sweet. We were told to stay inside, not to lick, not to inhale deeply. But what was "deeply"? How much unfiltered air was safe to breathe? I was never not reminded of precautions and safety, but all the same I had no problems breathing. I paid no attention to the warnings. I had nothing to do on the outside anyway.

I passed the day in the basement, in the one room clear of Harold's crates. The floor was heated concrete, with pillows and cushions along the walls. I sat propped on pillows with a table holding three monitors before me, each sending me a different stream. In the morning I toggled between chimp cams and video clips, lessons, and a wide-ranging assortment of feeds. When the air cleared a bit, Azzie and Celia came over. Each took a corner of the room. We kept the lights dim and we ingested V.

We each glowed in the light of our screens. We focused on what was before us. Screen glow felt like a heat lamp, like a hug, like a caress into pixelation. We consumed capsules filled with powders, we snorted and injected; we tracked how many hours, how many milligrams, how many half-lives existed in a day of ingesting. And we absorbed: instructional clips, dosing vlogs, CCTV streams, restreams, old films and really anything transferred digitally.

Celia followed a bird-watching drone cam and attempted to memorize the chemical properties of the top 200 supplements but ended up posting pouty selfies and obsessively checking Samsun's availability. Azzie streamed surgical cams, sex cams, and looked for hot boos in the ACCLIMATION feeds shared with third years across factory hubs. We wouldn't meet these students until our schooling was complete, and only then if we headed to university. Azzie bitched that our classmate Maxine was effusive, posting like she was in some state of post orgasmic bliss. I should've expected this. Maxine was my mother's protégé and at times assisted Dr. Billy. I resented that Maxine was taking to V. so readily.

I turned off two of my screens and watched old silent film clips. Black and white, outlines of tall city buildings, but mostly I liked to look at the faces and how much was communicated with a glance. Each twitch of the lip or batting of an eye was a meaningful gesture. My favorite was Joan of Arc's ecstasy, her gaze. The lone tear down her cheek, at the stake. It destroyed me, the way she was persecuted, the way she could overthrow armies and make priests quake. The way she enacted her vision and accepted her fate.

Later that evening, Harold was in his study when Judy pulled me aside. She said testing day was coming. That I was still not acting myself and that this was concerning. I pointed out that I was very much myself regardless of how she thought I should be acting. "Point taken," she'd said. But she had already concluded that I was suffering from the weight of things, of excesses. She sat beside me on the sofa as Esmerelda started pawing my lap. Judy explained that I had a wanting that would never leave and I carried this emptiness like a pocket within me. That this was normal, but if we ignored it, it would curl like a cat inside of me and grow. With augmentation it could be kept in control. Or rather, I could choose how it manifested.

I asked if she knew this feeling.

She nodded, yes.

I was surprised she was so candid. She said she saw life as a riddle she answered with methods to coordinate and simplify. She found meaning in reducing complications, untangling knots. This was so satisfying, she said, and now it had become as natural to her as breathing.

"What if I want something else?" I asked. I hated placation. "And who is this 'we'?"

She said, "Us, of course, we are a team..."

"What if keeping this empty pouch is important? Maybe it's a place for gestating."

She grimaced. "Hannah, please. I'm serious."

"I am too. I like having my cats," I said. I certainly liked Esmerelda on my lap even though she was now biting at my hand.

"Like them or not you'll need a way to tame them."

III.

It was almost as if our talk had quelled my cats, because I soon felt closer than I had to what I'd call normal. School days passed in chat flirtations. We exchanged IM's on animal mating. Shared images of screen-sized cocks and boxing matches and glitched animation. We downed energy drinks with augmentation, swallowed capsules filled with nutrients, all bio-manufactured at the factory. We recorded the days and nights of our screen lives: as in the constant glow on our faces, as in our constant palm gaze, as in the steady stream of a multiplicity of feeds (never fewer than three).

We were hooked up, jagged up, as always. We took our pills and powders during the designated times at school. We took in the fifteen minutes of morning salutation before first period, at the admin lab after second, then after third, the bell would ring and we'd head to the canteen, where we did our midday dosing.

We were greeted with audio recordings reminding us to take this seriously, to not make trades, to not dose defiantly, to not snort powders that were to be injected, etc., etc. Nourishment was available in pills and powders and in an assortment of e-lyte+ waters. We set up our devices to record as we sat side by side at one of three long tables, or at a smaller satellite table along the room's periphery. We measured doses and consumed and recorded our taking for our mothers and coaches, and for most of us that was Dr. Billy.

We took out our powders and straws and sniffed lines from the tables before us. We applied transdermal films that gave way to smooth expansion. Injections were swift and most effective. Though most of the time for most of us it was swallow swallow swallow.

Though no matter how much I swallowed I always felt empty. Even on better days, the cat inside was never satisfied. It clawed and grew beastly. Everyday blah was my new reality. I was passing time to what—to become another Judy? If I skipped a dose of V., I felt a bit more like who I used to be. There was a sense of warmth inside me. But even so I couldn't not take. Judy's defense: everyone benefits from chemical lift.

I didn't see how fact and matter mattered more than curiosity, investigating depth. I started investigations—gathered fragments of what I thought we'd forget, and what was already forgotten: how we are made of the same elements as stardust, storm clouds, tar pits.

We were offered a factory future only if we stayed at the top of the class. And if we wanted to leave Lumena Hills? These connections would come through the factory too. We were told dreams were to be used for envisioning futures and practical things, like managing a lab or engineering advanced dose delivery systems. Creativity? There was a pill for that too.

In these early days of third year, during this midday dosing, Celia introduced us to "shopping." She said it went like this, as we three sat at our usual table. She told us to flip open our titanium cases, slide open our crystalline organizers and we were to barter.

"Barter?" Azzie asked.

"Yeah, like you want to trade up."

"Ok, cool." I said, "but what about this?" I pointed to my device's lens. Our taking was monitored.

"You know they only spot-check these things."

"Then you don't know Judy."

Celia shrugged and said Samsun and his table of factory brats and bros had been doing this since day one and no one's onto them. "He says his dad and all the lead scientists explore off-label uses, so like, why shouldn't we?" She placed her device on the table so that it was capturing her face at an angle. She leaned forward, with her newly black hair falling forward, then took a bright orange Sunkiss in her palm. "Here's the trick," she said, and she held her palm to her mouth then swept it along her cheek, in one swift and brilliant gesture.

I tried this too with my V. and it really was so easy. Just move the capsule to my lips and along the side of my cheek, in one determined motion. I checked my replay even. Azzie watched us with some hesitation, until I placed my spare V. before her. Then she turned and placed a tab of Edge Eraser in Celia's palm, and Celia then passed her spare Sunkisses to me. These inevitably gave me a warm burst of energy through the afternoon.

More friends joined us the following day and days and this made for more possibilities of trades. I invited identical twins, Samuel and Linnaeus, who wore matching striped shirts and the same soundless soled shoes, Azzie brought her most recent crush Jeni, and Celia invited a fellow Buddhist named Doreen. I traded two magenta-and-black caps for Samuel's smaller turquoise jewels. Celia traded her orange horse pills for an ounce of Jeni's onyx elixir. Azzie gave her pink pearls for Doreen's jade ovals.

The exchange gave me a sense of control over something and a sense of relief. My inner cat didn't feel like it was scratching at me. I felt a purr, like I didn't feel panic when I went on to fourth period. My afternoon wasn't passed with gripped teeth. I did nod off a bit later in sixth, Power, Politics, and Leadership taught by Mr. Crawford, which despite my new calm energy, was still so incredibly tedious. Who were these rulers and why should *I* care about old school dictators? These kings and legislators and policy makers, these men of the world who had done whatever the fuck they pleased. They had so little to do with me.

IV. DOSING and MAINTENANCE

Testing day came later in the fourth week of classes. It usually affirmed what we already knew about our minds and their shapes, but this year with V., the stakes were higher. Starting V. could alter the shape of a mind, how it organized and retained information. Like a renovation. *Picture additions, new rooms, perhaps an additional floor*, Dr. Billy had said. He'd said our minds, like this structure, could form gaps and cracks which could lead to worse things when left unchecked. But he feigned the inability to list any of these things when asked. Instead, he'd reiterate the reasons we tested, which included:

Stop Gaps Before They Start
Spot Gaps Before Causing Problems
Find Hidden Cracks
Test for Hybrid / Altered Fruit Shapes and Integrity
Be Proactive

I saw this list projected onto the gym wall when I entered. I was handed a gown and given a number, then told to sit. The gym was filled with rows of small closet-sized tents. I distracted myself from thoughts of the test by looking at projections, which outlined the various fruits and their classifications. I had always been mid-apricot with pomegranate leanings. Apricots had integrity—their minds mastered what they stored with grace—although Judy was convinced that with VALEDICTORIAN I had pineapple potential. Or at least I'd be closer to and more competitive in the talent pool.

Mental type was classified by fruit shape. Dr. Billy said fruit made it easier to relate to what's inside, and besides, what's not to like about a pineapple, a kiwi, a mangosteen? The pumpkin and tomato minds were large and impenetrable, difficult to reach. Pomegranate minds were that of the worker bee, with one fact nestled against another in proximity until they formed a cluster. On V. the gray matter was made malleable and able to retain disparate facts: like Judy's birthday (*November 11*), Gramp's favorite book (*Moby Dick*), the Pythagorean theorem, better known as 'A squared plus B squared equals C squared,' a lengthy and lackluster description of entropy, as explained by Judy: *a clean house has a tendency towards dirty dishes and footprints and dust gathered, piles of books and empty cabinets and general disorder unless energy is turned inward*. When facts formed disparate connections, they grew into groups. Like apartment tenants they aligned for no other reason but proximity. With V. these minds sustained interconnections more readily.

When my number was called, I was directed to a tent where I was told to remove my clothes, put on the gown, and wait for an assistant. The assistant came in wearing silver scrubs and spotless white sneakers. He placed leads on my forehead, temples, and chest. He placed a swim cap with wires over my head. All of this without taking a breath. The wires were threaded down my back and connected. I then followed the assistant into another tent. I was accustomed to the process.

"Lie down," he said, motioning to a padded chair in recline. He took a vial and syringe. "Stings," he said, "just for a second," as he primed it. When he injected, the warmth spread out beyond my skin to fill the room.

I woke to sounds of a machine spitting feed. *Zzzzt Zzzzzzt Zzzzt.* High pitched. Felt like my head squeaked. My feet were numb, my mind iced. Dr. Billy stood above me looking pleased, yammering to the assistant who now stood to the side. I was sent to the next partition; its surfaces were reflective and bright. Dr. Billy's assistant entered a few minutes later. He smiled but his eyes held no expression. He said he had the results. I was a pineapple. On the cusp. I knew what this meant: stable foundations, structures in place, extreme capacity for acquisition and uptake. I changed back into my clothes and was released. I had mixed feelings about this, especially when Dr.

Billy raised his fist in the air to congratulate me on my way out.

I went back to my locker to gather my things. Classes were canceled for the afternoon and Azzie had texted me that she had ideas for what to do. My device vibrated. A message from Judy: kisses and pineapple emojis. And a second: she said she'd always known V. would work miracles for me.

Azzie ran up to me, pressed with impatience. "About time, you!" she said and dropped her bag. She leaned her backside against the locker so she could scrutinize those walking by. She'd done herself up. Mauve lips, foundation that made her zits less apparent, a black jean jumpsuit—it was a good look. She asked how my test went.

"Pure pineapple," I said with more enthusiasm than I felt.

She pressed my chest—"Me too! So this hell's been worth it?"

I shrugged.

"Okay, then. Forget about fruits." She turned to me and whispered, "I have an adventure for us." She explained she wanted me to accompany her on a trip to her ex's to steal back belongings she'd lent, which included a projector, her favorite jacket, and a chromium pillbox that had belonged to her father.

"You want me to help you break into your ex's house?"

"Not 'break into.' More like help retrieve my possessions. There's a difference. And I know for a fact no one will be there." Liesl had refused to acknowledge Azzie's calls and prostrations after she'd heard, correctly, that Azzie had been making out with a first year in the shower room.

I found Azzie irresistible when she begged me like this, but I knew she was very capable of handling herself. Besides, I wanted nothing to do with this kind of drama. I didn't give an answer. I took my pills from my case in the locker and swallowed them dry.

"Look, you don't even have to get out. Just ride with me and keep an eye out?" I paused, then agreed, and slammed my locker door.

That's when I heard a scream.

WTF? I said turning to Azzie, who looked as surprised as me. I saw people rushing from Ms. Tigue's classroom. The door was propped open. As I approached the threshold, I could see someone bending over Ms. Tigue's desk. On the floor I could make out a toppled chair and what looked like the shape of a body in it.

I saw Ms. Tigue's body on the floor seizing, her arm shaking, and her blonde hair in a pool of blood. I heard someone yell to call the paramedics. Azzie took off down the hall. I must've entered the room because suddenly I was standing over Ms. Tigue. She wasn't bleeding; her head was surrounded by magenta beads.

Were they pills? Were they pomegranate seeds? Until now I'd thought fruit shape was merely a heuristic, but now I saw with my own eyes the physicality of a pomegranate brain, that it was possible we were transforming our minds into fruit. What was Ms. Tigue doing on the floor?

It was possible she'd fully embodied her fruit and was ripe, overly. *There is special providence in the fall of a sparrow.* Soundbite: *Hamlet*—ran through my mind. I don't know why. All this time I just stood there looking at Tigue, her arm shaking on the floor, and then out the window at the factory on the hill, its stacks, the smoke ever rising. I thought of the weaver sparrow who no longer flew in that sky, extinct only weeks ago.

Next thing I knew, Crawford was leading me down the hall to Billy's office, which was frenzied and full of people. He took me to a side room with a chaise lounge and told me to rest my mind.

"Now's a fine time for that!" I protested.

"Calm down, close your eyes, breathe deeply. Think of something soft and welcoming." He handed me a warm compress and a glass of e-lyte+ water and sat down beside me. "I'm sorry you had to witness that... I've called your mother."

We sat in silence until Judy arrived. Judy's excitement about my pineapple results had faded, obvi. She hugged me and stroked my back, and I felt calmer though still on edge. She lamented, "I'm sorry, dear, I'm going to have to drop you at home and then turn around—they've called an emergency school board meeting." She assured me I wouldn't be alone for long. Harold would come home from work early.

It wasn't the alone time that bothered me, but more the awkwardness of Harold's attempts to allay my worries. I took my place in the basement and he took his in his study and later he called me up when dinner was ready. Harold stared out the window at the factory stacks as we ate our gluten and beans. We sat in silence and every so often he'd look toward me and open his mouth as if he were about to say something. His mouth would hang for a second, but then he'd fill it with another forkful, and look back toward the factory. The factory, like a panopticon, stood over this town. I'd always been calmed by this in some way knowing the factory, or at least its stacks, were visible from most windows, and a reminder the factory was humming away and helping keep the rhythm of our days. But now it felt more menacing, like it was dominating. I couldn't look at it without thinking of Ms. Tigue. I wanted to take an EmptEZ to forget. But I wasn't allowed to yet.

I started talking to Harold so he'd stop doing the thing with his mouth. Though once I started I couldn't stop: "The terrible sound, blood on my sneakers, stained by those awful seeds. The locker door slams. Someone screams. Why would she? On testing day of all days. The seeds, the pills, rolling on the ground. And her blonde hair, fallen from her head. Though it wasn't her blood—were they even pomegranate seeds?"

"Hannah, hon. Shhh. Stop. You're getting worked up."

I knew he was right. Instead I tried to concentrate on the thin lines of smoke rising from the stacks outside the window.

"I just don't get it...."

Harold mumbled, "Sometimes there's no reason."

I suspected something else. Like maybe Ms. Tigue wanted us to see the force that felled her. Whatever that was. I closed my eyes but all I saw was a halo of seeds around her head, her wig on the floor, her hand shaking weakly and pointing toward the hill.

Harold sat there nodding, opening his mouth into contortions but not saying a thing. He placed his hand on my shoulder, as if to reassure me.

Rumor had it that Ms. Tigue's head was filled with pomegranate seeds, and that when her chair tumbled over, her head had cracked open. This seemed true, I said, when asked by administrators, their assistants, my classmates, and neighbors. I was told the more I thought about the calamity the longer it would stay with me. But also, I was told to refrain from taking EmptEZ until they'd accessed all of my relevant memories. Their questions didn't stop and I had to keep answering. I was questioned by school authorities, by the factory's forensics team, by Dr. Billy's team of medical officers. There was an SOP they'd said. "A what?" I'd asked. A system of established procedures that we were following and this, they said, they hoped would reassure me.

I didn't need their reassurances. I needed to forget. I told the story so many times my memory seemed to morph. Sometimes I imagined I was sitting in Tigue's chair, sometimes I saw Celia, but never Azzie. Every time I conjured the scene I saw vials along the side of the desk, some toppled, a device dropped on the floor, screen cracked, Tigue's yellow hair fallen beside her. I'd connected the dots in my mind from her arm to the short fuzz on her head, to the toppled bottles on the ground, to round pills running like marbles. I was sure her skull had cracked open and pomegranate seeds had rolled out. I was told this hadn't happened, not quite. It couldn't have. But this was all I could envision.

It's so EZ to EMPTY your mind with *EmptEZ*

Plagued by negative thinking, bad memories, recurring dreams, replay of untoward interactions in a loop on repeat? It's never been EZ-er to wipe these hiccups away without setting yourself back.*

Take an EmptEZ – it's as EZ as pressing delete.

*EmptEZ has been proven not to impede exercise or development of mental capacity

V. CONTRAINDICATIONS

Judy scheduled my Cognitive Release for the end of the following week. The days between were long and terrible. School kept on and I felt a new sense of leaving my body whenever I took V.—as if this was not my hand before me toggling between screens, as if this was someone else's hair matted from not washing. I felt like I was drifting through each day, and days mattered only for getting through them. I wasn't in a good way. And yet Azzie somehow had emerged unscathed. Her explanation was that I took it all in, absorbed it. She was more resilient. She had run, she had acted. And then she'd run into Liesl in the halls and somehow they'd made amends. Maybe because it was in the wake of a tragedy. People do funny things. Liesl even apologized for being such a dick about holding Azzie's belongings hostage. They'd then gone together to retrieve Azzie's items and kissed each other's cheeks when she left.

When I listened to Azzie recount this story, I could hear her take pleasure in her cunning. Azzie sat beside me and I lay flat on a bed in a room devoid of light. I'd been ordered to spend my free period in one of the school's darkfulness rooms. This had been suggested as a way to counter my fraught nerves until my release. Azzie kept me company when she could. She generally spent the hour talking as my mind drifted.

But it's like Tigue haunted me. I thought of how she'd taught classes on design and complementarity. From her I'd learned about layouts and the golden ratio and Pantone and glitches. She wore brilliant platinum wigs and bright violet dresses and when she'd smiled her teeth gleamed. She'd always seemed so colorful. I'd taken that as happy.

We'd been told the school and factory together were investigating the reasons for her collapse. Physically she was fine but her mind remained sandwiched somewhere between vegetative and alive. Everyone had ideas of why: overdose, misuse, emotional and mental lability. Some even claimed she'd done it to go on disability. She'd left no note and no one was close enough to remark on whether she'd been off of late. The blame and inquiry was directed at her, what she'd done. No one asked if what had happened was the factory's fault. I noted this to myself. I added Ms. Tigue to the endangered species list even though she wasn't a species.

I hadn't witnessed anything like this before. I knew of a handful of students who'd had to leave school because of issues with their supplements. It wasn't talked about in any definitive terms. Azzie had shared that a lot of them ended up in the hospital's psych unit. She'd learned this from her mother,

Trinie, who was a nurse on one of the general floors.

Judy encouraged me to do more work with my hands during this time. She thought it might help ground me. Rummaging through the basement didn't count, nor did messaging. Maybe I could learn to knit, she suggested. Just the basics. And it was something I could do while watching video clips. This seemed funky, kind of old timey, and so unlike Judy to suggest. Needless to say I liked the idea. What I ended up making looked mostly like chain links and unwieldy beehives. Judy said it wasn't the end state that mattered but that I was using my hands and soothing my mind.

On the morning of the release, I wore my favorite white wingtips. Dr. Billy had cautioned that colors surrounding me during the process could have profound effects. Judy drove me to Dr. Billy's private office, the one I'd never visited. It was located in a tower of medical offices across the street from the hospital and connected to it via a pedestrian bridge. The building itself seemed to be made mostly of windows. Judy dropped me off out front and told me to take the elevator to the fifth floor. Dr. Billy greeted me at the office door. He was wearing a lab coat over his white-and-gray sweater covered with little triangles and his silver laceless shoes. The office was empty except for us. He spoke to me in almost a whisper. Silence was important, he stressed, as he led me back through the corridors. We entered a room the size of Judy's walk-in closet. The walls and floors were tiled, and all surfaces seemed to glow.

"Lie down on this," he instructed while pointing to a recliner. There was something placid about him today. His upbeat attitude was more muted. I liked this side of Billy better, even if he was just attempting to set the right mood. He gave me some capsules to swallow and a small cup of water to wash them down. He then placed sensors on my forehead and behind my ears and on my ankles too. He handed me a swimmer's cap, like the one from testing day, and told me to put it on. I closed my eyes. I could feel him tightening the wires. He told me it was important that I remain calm throughout this process. Something in the determined way he did this made me feel assured too. Though from what I gathered Billy was all surface; there was nothing below. He then handed me a cup of warm yellow sludge to drink. I gagged. It was clumpy.

The room was a womb of warmth and light. I closed my eyes again and this time Dr. Billy sounded distant. He asked me to conjure memories and focus on specific details, to play them back chronologically. I queued to the last moment I remembered before the calamity: closing my locker door, Azzie's smirk as she told me the story about kissing in the shower room. About Liesl finding out and not talking to her, about needing to retrieve the projector and the pill box. Then the scream.

"That's good," he said calmly.

My body jumped when he said this. I wasn't talking aloud, I didn't think.

"Breathe slowly," he said. "Calmer. Concentrate."

"I'm trying."

"Good. Now. Reexamine each detail with the most attentiveness."

The scream brought forth the fluorescent light reflected on the desk, bringing forth the dirty daisy wig against the deep red. Pomegranate seeds falling like rain around me and I am hiding in a bus shelter as the wind blows the seeds, now pelting down on my shoes and pants. A pool of violet liquid rises around my feet. I am hiding under a checkered quilt in my bed. Dispensary shelves filled with tiny elephants, their beady eyes following me. I am wearing Tigue's wig and a set of false teeth. I pull out the teeth—they don't belong to me. I am panicky.

"You're doing so well. Just a little longer to complete."

I tried to do as I was told.

Suddenly a drain opened—I'm not sure if that's the best way to describe it? There was color swirling away into whiteness. I was neck-deep in a bathtub filled with blood, turning into brilliant orange and then green like seaweed, all color flowing into a stream, the stream circling and disappearing.

I opened my eyes.

Dr. Billy stood before me. I looked up and for once I was relieved to see his face, his gray eyes, his silver curls. He was looking at me so warmly. I wondered if maybe I had always misjudged his rude ebullience.

It felt like a large hole had opened inside of me.

"Don't think. Just breathe."

An indefinite period; centuries, maybe.

And then a gentle touch on my shoulder.

Judy sat beside me petting my hair, tucking a wisp behind my ear. "You're a trooper sweetie. You're going to feel so much better soon."

VI. USE IN ACADEMIC SETTINGS

When posed the question, *How to explain our presence within the universe?* students recited contradictory proofs, though most often they cited the donut theory based on data from Mather & Smoot: geometric principles applied described the universe as a disc with its center missing. Passageways within made multiple interconnections; they folded into themselves like the fissures in a brain, but infinitely expanding.

A donut with gaps is also how I pictured my mind looked after Cognitive Release. When I attempted to recall memories associated with testing day and Ms. Tigue, I found I no longer could. I could still access most relevant facts though I had a vague sense—was it muscle memory?—of an absence. Sometimes I could coax details from hiding though of course I was not supposed to be trying. It was like glimpsing the silhouette of a chimp or watching a movie all glitched.

I spent more time on my own after this. Azzie was always drifting, moving from crush to crush. I called it brachiation. She'd achieved a state where she could go from one crush to another without losing momentum. This began to bother me, the way she always craved the attention of someone new. The way she still had access to her emotions and desires, even on V. She spent so much of her time with Jeni, who was a year ahead of us, and possessed some rare kind of fruit mind, like a citrus mixed with mangosteen. She was eccentric, wore her hair in a bob and bright lipstick in a different shade each day. She wore lots of colors and leggings as pants. She had studied closely with Ms. Tigue, which I thought we'd maybe bond over, but now that I'd had my Release, it was an awkward reminder of what I could no longer recollect. And Jeni had her own lunch table of trades. Azzie started lunching with them, and around the two of them I felt like an appendage, like a thumb drive filled with files from an outdated operating system. They would talk over me, flirting. And besides, no one at that table wanted to give me their relaxants. And Celia was off fluttering around Samsun on the other side of the canteen.

I passed entire days without uttering a word. This wasn't a decision I'd made. I felt like a wraith drifting through days, in communion only with my soundbites, clips, and screens. Even my chimp family had left. The chimp feed now showed vacant landscape—trees and dirt and the lake that changed only with the light of the day. I missed watching the girls gang up on their brother and spying on the interloper. I realized now I'd known next to nothing about them besides their coordinates and their dramas and daily habits. I didn't know if what appeared on my section of screen was their home or a stop along the way, if they were dead or if they'd migrated.

Still, I always had my pill case with me, with a vial of V., extended release. I took one twice daily, as well as the tablets I'd dose throughout the day. I stayed away from injections and concentrates and anything too high maintenance. I had a vast array of powders to dissolve and to snort and to cut with other powders, vials to sniff and inhale. And I had an arsenal of relaxants. Sublingual strips of Mental Floss to help organize thoughts, Liquid EnerG for boosts, and ampules of FortiFYI and Meniscus, which helped forge connections and mental agility. My dosing schedule changed weekly, sometimes daily, with my new lability. My daily dosing record was rarely the same on consecutive days but looked something like:

VALEDICTORIAN	28mg XR capsules x x
	2.5mg IR tabs x x _ x _ _ + ½
MENTAL FLOSS	10mg strips x x x
ENERG (LIQUID)	4 oz. ✓✓
FORTIFYI	17.5 gm powder inhaler x _ x
MENISCUS (powder)	_ _ _ _
ANXIETEZ	21mg ER patch ✓ (day 5 of 7)
SUNKISS	2mg capsules _ _ _ xxx xxx
DELIXIR (powder)	x x x x x

I'd arrive at school, take during morning salutation and move from class to class as the bells and vibrations told me to. Morning salutation for pineapples was a quiet room filled with only a chorus of *wahwah-sush*, *wawah-sush*, the susurration of constant release. I was now one of them—the ambitious kids, the factory brats and bros, including Samsun and his friends. I didn't care much for them. Pineapples were the type to carry ampules of V. concentrate in their bags, along with sets of weights and scales. They walked with administration machines mounted to abdomens, slipped into pockets, inserted under skin, in an attempt to reach steady state.

As a pineapple I was supposed to take my role seriously. "Manifest destiny of the mind" was a refrain reserved for us. Azzie seemed to relish this new authority. Though Azzie and I were distinct from the pineapples who had always been or had aspired to be, like Maxine who praised her supplements with the intensity of an evangelist. But Azzie and Maxine were immune to the ways V. fucked with me. I thought Celia was lucky to have not made the cutoff. V. mattered less for the other fruits, as in it didn't affect their minds in the same way, and as a result they generally weren't as awful or anal in their pursuit of steady state.

"How do I distinguish between what's me and what's chemical?" I asked Harold one night, one of the few I spent with him in his study. When I was younger, he'd placed a velour reading chair in the corner that I still claimed as my own. I sat with him less often now, but it was still one of my favorite places and one the few where Judy didn't bother me.

His answer: "No difference."

"Not helpful."

"Sorry?" He seemed unsure of his words more than the sentiment.

We sat in silence as I gazed at his desktop covered in books and instruments of measurement like the compass with a stylus that he used to draw circles on his screens and measure planetary widths and distances. There were a series of telescopic lenses, and behind him, crates full of reference texts.

He said my generation would become experts in storage and integration, and to do this we'd need to distance ourselves further from our animal natures. We were to consume and continue. He said pasts and potential only mattered in the way they were used. Harold didn't believe in the subjunctive tense of *could* and *should* and *ought to.*

He didn't say it that evening but he'd told me over and over so many times before that I heard him say it in my mind. I could recite his words, or if not his words, his sentiment:

We are a series of chemicals and atoms and signals, moving forward in time. Always yearning for dissolution, release, all the while fighting to not do this. Perception is subjective and skewed.

The biggest question? Consciousness—what is it, how to maneuver through, tap into? Chemical betterment. It's one way to go. It's what you're born into, you really have no choice.

There was only so much room within a skull. When capacity was exceeded, information spilled. I imagined it resembled the factory smokestacks spilling into the sky and rolling over us, accumulating in drifts. I wished theories of awareness were more valued, that the gravity of our situation was acknowledged—not gravity in the sense of pulling our bodies closer to the earth, but in the weight of our future, with augmentation and its contraindications.

/**MENTAL*FLOSS**/ Night-sky atrophy. Telescopes numbered one through ten, the largest fitted with a 12-inch lens. Just how far has the light traveled, with supernova energy as strong as 100 million earths exploding simultaneously. **MENTAL*FLOSS** connects one two three four—draws lines like a delicate string connecting stars to night to sky in space over time freeing the constellation within your mind.

VII.

Around this time in Crawford's class, we learned about death masks, how in ancient societies making them was a common practice used to preserve the faces of family members, a memento mori. Patricians, rulers and kings would have their faces recorded—they'd be painted and molded and busts would be sculpted to record the face upon death. The images I saw were all of old men, balding, eyes blank. I was fascinated by the tactile way these masks were made. I could do this for Ms. Tigue, I thought, stage a recreation at least, and I could do this for my friends. We weren't dying yet, but we all would. I decided I wanted to document our lives not for posterity—I didn't believe in that—but because we too had existed.

I used a pair of gloves that had been adapted to record sensory input. They were dark gray and rubberlike with nodes on the fingers' undersides. They had wires like veins that ran over the top, and I jerry-rigged them to manipulate the colors and textures that resulted on the monitor.

Azzie sat for me first. We sat outside on the stoop in front of her house, as I pulled the gloves over my hands.

"They look like finger condoms," she joked.

Azzie made the most vivid expressions, even as I passed my hands over her face. I traced the curve of her forehead, ran my palm from the corner of one eye over the bridge of her nose, over the stud in her lip, and below her round chin.

"It doesn't look like me!" she complained when I showed her image. It was a series of blue streaks, with eddies of green bleeding into yellow. But I saw her in it. More than any photo or selfie or representation, it captured her depth. She wanted me to erase it but I refused. "Baby's first headshot," I said in jest.

She said she wanted to try the gloves on me. I tried to say no but she insisted. I closed my eyes as she held my cheeks, ran her fingers over my forehead, nose, chin, then down the base of my neck. When she was finished, I saw a pale yellow square offset by sea green and burnt orange across the bottom. In it all I could see was the flat screen amplifying flatness within me.

These portraits became an obsession, not just with touch and colors and making but with other peoples' faces: cheekbones in so many variations, brows, deep-set eyes, pursed lips, dimpled chins. I walked through crowds and wondered how the shape of each face would translate onto my screen. I'd be struck by an especially strong brow or the way some people walked around as if they had sour candy in their mouth. I became bolder.

I stopped people on the street and asked if they'd be willing to sit for me. I was surprised by how many agreed to do this on the spot when asked, though far fewer responded when I reached out later for follow-up. Soon I was making ten portraits a week. I did Judy's (*narrow, pointed, predominant colors: beige and cornflower blue*) and Harold's too (*empty yet full, pale green and cloud shaped*). I did Azzie's face again and again. Faces on V. were usually vacant but not Azzie's. Somehow hers always surprised me. It might be something as small as the curl of her lip, her open-mouthed laugh.

Celia's face was softer, rounder, and sweet, but also her portraits revealed dark crevices that I wouldn't have expected. I saw Azzie's unapologetic boldness and Celia's soft recklessness. My own portraits turned out closer to Celia's but I wished they were closer to Azzie's. I mean sometimes I wanted to fall into Azzie's blue curls and sometimes I wished I could be her.

I did one of Crawford—his face seemed rid of its anxiety, his determination wasn't present in it. And I did one of Maxine, at her request. Maxine had a bold, bold mouth. I was surprised by the intensity of her lips. I touched and opened them. She smiled, then relaxed. Her second portrait held that.

How beautiful our bodies were.

I started doing a series of self-portraits, too, legs

and arms, torso and clit—I hung them on a line strung across my room. It was the only way to see myself from a distance.

What was the shape of me? I still felt so much vacancy. But with my portraits hanging, the answer was obvious—

VIII. PHYSICAL MANIFESTATIONS

Azzie texted to say she needed a companion for focus. I never knew what to expect when I received these texts. Sometimes the house was empty but more often there'd be a small crowd waiting. This time when I arrived, she gave me a kiss on the cheek and whispered that Celia was in a way. I followed her downstairs and Celia was there, curled on the couch.

Azzie sat down beside her. "He's not worth this kind of mental spin," she said and handed Celia a canary yellow tab. She then placed one in my hand and took another for herself. I swallowed mine and sat down on the mat on the floor facing them. Azzie cued the lights to dim. Celia was restless. She sat up, grabbed the vial, and tapped two more tabs of Tranquile into her palm. She paced the room, then took a third and washed it down with a mouth of e-lyte+ water.

"Fuck him," she said. "I mean, I fucking…" She stopped mid-sentence and just stared at the light. She twisted the antler from the chain on her neck and inhaled a pinch. I'd never seen her like this. "Oh Hannah, Azu," she said. "You know I've been with him, sitting with his table, ingesting after school, and he didn't judge when I didn't make pineapple. I was feeling really bad, you know... anyway... we were studying energetic properties between bodies and endogenous chemical release."

"I'm sure you were," I laughed, then saw her face slip.

"I thought he was into me."

"He was, obvi," I said.

"Yeah but, you know, we took D at his father's place. He asked if I wanted to try the outdoor sauna, and obvi yes. So we sat there in the wood house on the hot bench in our towels, steam around us, and he moved up on me. We start kissing, all that. He asked if he could put it in and in the moment, you know, the way he asked was so matter-of-fact. I don't even know what you'd call it. We fucked—maybe?"

"How can you *not* know?" Azzie looked perplexed.

"It was so good but so bad," she said, half laughing. "Like diving for clams. I ended up with a mouthful of sand." The way she described it I imagined their skin slipping over each other like whales, the way their mouths mingled, lingering, the hardness of his cock, long and oddly thin. She said it hung at an angle. She was so soft and small and his body so tall and scrawny, that when I tried to imagine them side by side it seemed like he would pierce through her.

"XY's are so primal," I said, "and not in a good way. Like they have this latent desire for the hunt and kill."

Azzie glared at me and mouthed "STOP."

"Really though," Celia continued. "He was just squirm and done. I was like, 'What? Keep on!'" Afterward, when they dressed, he gave her a lame one-arm embrace and walked out to clean up and didn't return. She went inside and found him playing some zombie game on his device. Now he wouldn't respond to her messages. And of all things, she worried *she'd* done something.

"No response is the worst," she said. "It's killing me." Her face was puffy and she was wearing comfort gear, flannel pants with hearts and bears, a black tee with a pink teardrop between the breasts, and her black hair was impressively a mess. I thought she looked gorgeous, though this was not the usual Celia look.

I blamed stupid hominid mating habits. Immature males of the primate species haven't learned social responsibility. They're focused on conquering because that's what they're rewarded for. Celia had all of those endorphins kicking in. I wondered if maybe she should take some uppers even? Not that I knew. I just hoped the Tranquile kicked in soon.

"He's just a kiwi apple with a dad on the factory board," Azzie said. "No way he would test into pineapple on his own."

Celia feigned a smile. It was no use trying to placate this away.

We discussed inflicting some form of humiliation—which wasn't recommended by most of the advice-offerers online, *use at your own discretion* they said—but there were copious how-to's, Q&A's, message boards addressing this. Where would it take place—IRL or online? Had the to-be-shamed sexted photos? Were there sex shots, videos even? Gif & Post was promising—the limpdick.gif, cumface.gif etc. etc. were more effective when 1) his face appeared in the image, 2) he had a look of shame, and 3) the message was stated clearly.

Our potential methods included hacking other screens and networks, cracking LCD ad boards, and posting. The IRL options were more limited. What was his weakness? Knowing and exploiting this was central to using this method. Celia gave a list: he was embarrassed by his bad skin, he had a bad body image, and he resented people for assuming that his academic success was due to his father's position. His parents were on Lumena's board—but this wasn't a weakness. It meant he had access to and consumed extraordinary amounts of Delixir, and really any supplement he wanted.

What was his weakness though—lack of empathy? Was this a weakness even? It seemed to serve so many people so well. I pointed out that we could exploit it in the sense that he'd never anticipate a confrontation.

Azzie promised not to be aggressive, to not call too much of the wrong kind of attention. That was Celia's request, when we decided to do an intervention the coming Friday at the VR cage. Depending on how this went, we'd follow it by hacking into the local network and post some GIFs to humiliate him. Celia was reluctant but she soon agreed, as long as we promised to let her take the lead. The way I saw it we could help her reclaim some of the ground she'd lost. She seemed to think of this as an acceleration of karmic payback (though karma, as I understood it, was a life force, situated beyond ourselves, one that the universe enacted, not something that we could claim, but I stayed quiet). To help Celia was not only to vindicate her but reclaim some of that lost pussy power (her new sign off was 'sad meow =ˆ.ˆ/=').

Celia said she envisioned this as a subtle and graceful action, like a dance. We'd make Samsun wonder what had happened and worry about what would come next. She said she didn't need to stoop to traditionally male methods of domination. I was proud of her for thinking this—I knew it had to do with my chimp obsession and what she'd gleaned about their need for dominance. I knew if she used this intervention correctly, she, and through her, we could be like bonobos, and word would spread to give power to our shunning.

When I came home, I couldn't sleep—a paradoxical

effect of the Tranquile, I guess—and soon I found myself drifting deeper into a sea of links. I read about the bonobos, how they shared food and groomed each other after they'd just met, regardless of gender. Bonobos, I found, were the least touted species of apes despite this—I wish we humans had evolved in the same ways of caretaking. Of the primates they were the most peaceful, openly sexual, and generous. I found a link at the bottom of the screen to reportage on the last days of the bobcats, who were felled by a combination of a vicious mange that made many waste away and toxins in their prey. The result was an incredible uptick in rabbit populations, now that they were down a predator. I clicked through to a slew of stories about the piles of rabbit poop accumulating (*fertilizer seemed to be the best use*), how rabbits were burrowing into pits across the prairie, taking over abandoned basements, and ravaging fields of grass. I thought of Celia and Samsun ravaging her in the sauna, its humidity like a tropical forest. Why was the word for hot sex destructive and assumed the power to be masculine? And if the sex wasn't even good, and she didn't know if it happened, I didn't see how it could count. I just wish he'd been civil. But now Celia was raw like a nerve. She'd said she'd been downing handfuls of EmptEZ, and I searched for "best ways to acclimate mood" and "bad experience." I read that you should take an EmptEZ, and only one, optimally, within forty-eight hours to counteract negative affect. Follow up with a second dose a week later. This was supposed to temper feelings of disappointment and rejection, to sever feelings of attachment. And yet, it hadn't. So far it seemed to have had no effect.

IX.

The Lumena Center didn't do much for me ever, and on a Friday night especially, with all of its fluorescent lights illuminating the worst in the shoppers and supplement poppers and gamers and everyone moving within. Samsun was a habitué of the Center's VR cage, where guys, mostly, would play games wearing headsets, each assigned to a different padded cubicle. This abutted a literal cage where people gamed together and one of the challenges was not running into one another. In the last cage, people threw axes at life-size outlines of bodies projected onto a wall. This was justified as physical exercise, somehow, that helped sublimate aggressive tendencies or something like that. Samsun came here most Fridays, Celia had said. And we had vowed to help Celia avenge her sadness and what had become our mutual anger at his postfuck weirdness.

The Center had dispensaries at both ends with moving walkways spanning the distance between them. Between, there were kiosks for magnetic resonance and mental reset techniques and sign-ups for electrostimulation rooms. There were dosing hubs and recharge stations. People came on Friday evenings after school, after the factory's second shift, though I never understood why so many people were drawn to come here at the same time, as if being in a crowd was an experience they desired.

I met Celia and Azzie on one end of the second-floor walkway. When together we became a we in a way that made us stronger, bolder, a blur. Celia had done her hair up in braids that circled her head. She wore plastic fangs and a billowy see-through dress. She wore all black and a fanny pack. She had this new hand tremor too. When I asked her about it she laughed, said the EmptEZ had only made her cranky and shook her, literally. She'd been clawing walls ever since.

Azzie wore a bomber jacket and combat boots. I went for a more discreet, undercover look: black turtleneck and pants, augmented clear plastic framed glasses that could record my path of vision. Celia passed her antler around and we each took turns sniffing its Insta_Pleasure and licking our fingers for luck.

I queued the TrackHer®. It said Samsun was moving dynamically through the VR cage. We split up, turned our cameras to record, and took separate paths toward his location. I went zigzag between the walkways, checking the others' locations frequently. Celia moved more fluidly from side to side almost as if in doing so she were delaying the inevitable encounter. Azzie beelined and found Samsun first. He was checking into the ax throwing side, waiting on gear. He stood captivated by his device and unaware of her encroachment, Azzie said.

"Oh wait, eye contact made," she noted. I couldn't see the feed of what was happening, but I heard his mumble of a greeting and Azzie starting to rant: "Don't 'hi' me like we're friends. You're too busy throwing axes to respond to texts?" I paused to look at Celia's stream. It looked like she was detouring.

This wasn't how we'd planned it, but I knew of no other way forward so I carried on. Azzie and Samsun were in a stalemate. Behind them was a desk and behind that a man holding an ax. I saw Samsun's confused face and Azzie up in it, looking like she was about to bite his head off.

"You know, it's pretty shitty that you won't return Celia's messages," I told Samsun.

He was like, "Chill guys, you definitely need to reset."

Azzie started in again, "Don't 'guy' me either. You fuck with Celia, you fuck with us." She threw her chest up against his and stared him down.

He took two steps back, threw up his arms, and was like, "What the fuck!?"

I grabbed Azzie and pulled her back. She panted at me, that she was just about to launch into him. I told her she was lucky I'd stepped in as I gazed at the guys in the cage just beyond us, wandering blindly in a realm that made sense only to them. They had headsets covering their eyes, devices in hand, cords tethering them to the mainframe like umbilical cords.

"Abort, abort," I shouted into my device. Where was Celia? She'd turned off her camera though she still had audio on. "Celia. Meet us in the second-floor women's bathroom."

We took a moment and headed across the way, and entered the powder room, where we sat on the floor.

"Azzie," I chided, "I wouldn't call that subtle..."

"You didn't see the look he gave me."

"You deviated."

"You think she's pissed?"

"I mean, she's not responding." I messaged Celia: *Where are u? Not showing on the device. Come, come. A. says she's sorry.*

We decided to get on with the part deux. Next step was to hack into the local LED signage network and transmit Samsun's Ihaznodick.gif across it. It wasn't even a dick shot, just a series of images of him dressed head to foot in black, his slinky body fading into the dark corner, with a bright light above washing out his sad, sad face. It made him look isolated. There might have been a tear in his eye.

"She can always say she wasn't involved or some shit."

"You think?"

"I was just trying to empower her."

"You could've let her lead, you know? Let her slap his face, pull his hair, have a physical confrontation."

I sensed Azzie was really the one who'd wanted this. It was the male chimp who would show aggression, not the female, not the bonobo. Azzie had some real dick-related anger of late. Like she wanted to be the dominant male. I couldn't help but think of her father, still missing after so many years and the weight that had on her. She wouldn't talk about him, ever. I knew from Judy that he just got in his truck one day and never showed up to pick up his haul, never returned to Lumena Hills. His truck was found abandoned at a rest stop. No trace of him. No sign of foul play. Azzie changed the subject if it ever came up. But perhaps if we regressed, she'd be able to claim some form of dominance and heal.

People came and went as we sat there in the powder room attempting to hack into the local network. We moved to two plush chairs with a table between, its smooth self-cleaning surface used for cutting powders, organizing doses. Some girls lingered, but most came and went, passing the mirror, pulling hair, licking teeth, applying rouge, sniffing vials, taking cases from their purses and placing pills in their cheeks.

The fluorescent lights made my head scream.

No word still from Celia. My attempt to hack the

network wasn't working.

Azzie said she'd try.

I queued Celia's camera feed. She'd turned it back on. It was static. All I saw were a series of induction pots hanging.

"Something's wrong," I told Azzie. "Looks like she's in kitchenware."

"Sure, yeah this isn't working. Let's go find her." Azzie dug her hand into her pack and pulled out a tiny plastic banana and split it in half. She tapped out a palmful of pink tablets, swallowed one, held her palm to me. "Edge Eraser?" she offered.

I took one and then we left. We walked through a side door into the store showroom, past a series of screens and speakers and signal amplifiers, accessories like earpieces, headsets, glasses, helmets. We followed a maze to and through women's samples—formal dresses with elaborate brocades, others cut in modern shapes, boxlike and awful. Like, who would even wear these? We went on to lingerie, panties, and peek-a-boo nighties, we pushed through silks, pulled them through our fingers and held them to our faces, then headed to kitchenware.

I looked again at the camera stream and Celia's display. I saw two sets of legs, one from the feet up, and the other squatting, with knees pointed at the camera.

In front of us, there were two guards, one standing

over a counter and the other crouching under. I saw Celia's phone on the floor.

I asked the standing guard if he'd seen Celia. I described her black hair, braids, and billowy dress.

"Fangs?" he said.

"Yes."

He nodded and pointed toward the display of knives. They were shiny and sharp and strapped down. The other guard pointed to the door. "She went that way." He said he'd walked up as she was attempting to break a knife from the case. She had dropped the knife and run away.

"You just let her run?"

"Look, I tried to see if she was okay."

I grabbed Celia's phone from the floor and we took off, dodging perfume bots attempting sprays. The sky outside was dark with clouds and rain was pouring over the line of vehicles exiting.

We decided to split up and canvass the parking lot.

"No flaking," Azzie said.

"Yeah, no kidding."

I walked past the loading docks on the backside. On the other side, I saw a tiny woman standing by the side entrance. With her tiny fingers she held a tiny kerchief over her head. She looked observant and very wet.

I asked if she'd maybe seen Celia: "Braids, black dress, perhaps a bit discombobulated?"

She seemed to have trouble with her words. Her phrases came in spurts: "A particular...? I cannot tell.... Honestly... you look, nice girl..."

She was no help. I walked back toward the loading docks.

In the distance, I thought I made out Celia's outline walking in the lot. She looked lost. Her hair was soaked. She was walking along a row of parked cars back toward the Center, toward me. She tripped and stumbled and all of a sudden her body launched into the air, she flew forward, and into the path of a sports utility vehicle.

The sports utility vehicle halted and I started running. I watched Celia fall so slowly—her shoulder hit its grill and then she crumpled, it seemed, into a heap on the ground. I ran over to her side and kneeled beside her. The sports utility vehicle's lights made her look ghastly, her billow wilted, her pale skin damp. She looked like she was crying but it might've been the rain on her face.

"What's going on Cici? Tell me you're okay...?"

This didn't seem to register. She had a cut on her chin and her braids had fallen though that looked like the extent of her injuries.

The SUV driver was still in her car. Her shocked O of a mouth made her look like she was hyperventilating, with two screaming kids beside her. Finally she popped her door and ran over, and was like, "Are you trying to give me a heart attack or what?"

"Lady, look, I think she's hurt."

She just freaked. "Oh god it's not my fault. She hit us. We had no velocity and now just look at her." She took a capsule from her pocket and put it under her tongue. I had no time for her hysterics, to wait for it to kick in. I grabbed Celia's hand and tried to help her up but she was dead weight. The cars were lining up. I sent a location pin to Azzie and told her to get out here and quick.

"I'm calling an ambulance," the SUV driver said.

"No, no don't do that..." I turned to Celia, wanting her to agree, but she lay there, her eyes wide and without expression.

The woman was already talking to someone on her device. The children in the SUV started pressing their faces into the windshield, putting their mouths on the glass, and then turning the headlights on and off. The woman said paramedics were on their way, then went back to sedate her little monsters, or so I hoped. They were acting like little cretins whose behavior was so beyond. Judy would've had a field day with them.

Azzie came running just as the ambulance pulled up. She and I stood to the side as the EMTs asked Celia a long list of questions. They asked her to hold up one finger for yes, two for no. She could do this. They pressed their gloved hands over her body. I wondered what shape it would've made if they'd been wearing my gloves. They pulled her dress down to rub her chest. They needled and masked her and then lifted her onto a stretcher.

Azzie asked, "What's going on?"

The tall one said, "I can't conjecture. Nothing apparent. No contusions, no lacerations, no pupil dilation." They needed to run tests. She said it was standard procedure and lifted the back end of the stretcher into the ambulance. I attempted to climb in after them but she blocked me.

"Uh-uh! You can't ride."

"Just me?" I pleaded.

"No minors," she barked. But she seemed to take pity. "Sorry, not my rules. We're taking her to the Downtown Hospital. You can check on her there. Her guardians have been alerted."

The ambulance drove off, its lights rotating, the sound blaring, and the traffic again started moving. Azzie and I stood there watching, the rain running down our faces.

We walked back into the warm and dry of the Lumena Center feeling defeated. It was emptier near closing time, and we stood in the glare of its lights. I suggested we get a ride to the ER—though Azzie said it was pointless. They wouldn't let us in without Celia's mother's permission. And besides, it takes so long for them to do anything there. She said Celia would be placed in a tiny room where she'd be poked and needled even more, and there'd be just enough room in that room for Celia and her mother. "I'll call my mom," she offered. "Ask her to keep an eye out for Celia, you know, keep us posted on what's going on."

The Med Rx dispensary's counter was still packed. Its walls were so clean and bright, and between those walls were so many bodies. The bodies on the other side of the counter wore form-fitting suits and swept pills across plates with long, blunt knives. They used scales to measure powders, tapped powders into capsules. They mixed herbs and emollients with long butter knives.

The line was so long for made-to-order so we made a beeline for the machine. We tapped the screen for the round orange balls, SunKisses. Two grams of In-sta_Pleasure, a focus enhancer, and a purple pellet relaxant.

We took the Delixir, too. What was left. Three tablets. It was enough for the night.

If god is a chemical, swallowing is a prayer.
A pill is an answer. An exorcism. A placation.
Sometimes it's all.

X.

We took the bus back to Azzie's house, then sat in silence and stared out into the blank night. I took some Sunkisses while Azzie sat and texted with some girl. I started to feel the warmth of the pill kick in but it didn't offset the reel replaying in my mind: Celia tumbling into the SUV's grill, the collision that wasn't much of a collision. It only grew worse as I felt more relaxed. I saw Celia in Tigue's purple dress flashing me a Cheshire grin with her ultra-white teeth and then hitting the grille of the SUV. I was so vexed that our intervention had backfired and so incredibly. I was beset with so many if's—like if only Azzie had kept her mouth shut, or if we'd stopped when Celia changed course.

Azzie's eyes got so big when I told her this. "It's not like I shoved her in front of that car, you know."

I knew. I'd watched it. It was like she was on autopilot. "But if only we could figure it out. Like why she tried to steal the knife—did she want to initiate violence? With whom? And if so, who disgraced her more, Samsun or us?"

"Or none of the above. Don't be so dramatic. We'll ask her when she gets out."

"I can't stop seeing it: how she stumbled, then

retracted. Like a turtle pulling into its shell."

"... or a massive hard drive failure."

"Don't say that."

"Look," Azzie said, " Maybe it was too much. But don't hold the blade to your neck. Or to mine either."

She was right. I wanted someone to blame for the evening and how it had turned. Azzie took out the dispensary bag, then handed a glassine envelope to me. "I'd say it's time for these."

I opened the envelope, gave her one small tablet, a mellow purple with a "~d~" stamped on one side. I took another out, placed it under my tongue and let it dissolve.

Still I worried we were betraying Celia by not working harder to piece together what had happened and uncover what had fallen away—like if I could pinpoint that instant, then I could go back and make it different. But I knew no amount of attention could do that, attention to her, attention to my hand resting right here in front of me, attention to the loosening inside of me. A sudden warmth washed over me, and I started to sink into the couch.

Soon I was steeped in mellow. I could sense beauty in the way my feet inched across the thick carpet, in the way Azzie's toes curled at rest and the pout on the right side of her mouth, in the tenacity with which the couch embraced us, in the series of screens casting silver light across the room and beyond the window in the smoke rising from the factory stacks then sinking into a fog that coated the trees.

Azzie's girl Jeni texted. Said the rooftop party that had been on hold during the rain was now on. We set out together, stumbled through the streets, past house after house with nearly identical faces: door on the right, windowpane on the upper left, a second floor with a dormer window. These fronts were large and familiar, the streets were so soft and somber. I looked into the rooms that still had lights on and imagined my life unfolding within them.

Here wasn't much different than down the block. But the houses led to storefronts and soon we were on the edge of town that I didn't visit often. We walked past lots filled with metal pipes and lumber, backhoes and dump trucks. Soon we came upon buildings that were taller and skinnier. This was where the service workers lived, the custodial staff and contract workers, the artisans and envelope sealers. We reached a series of apartment buildings, stark red and reaching upward, twenty stories high. We arrived at a tall black gate. Azzie punched in a code and we took the elevator to the top, then climbed another set of stairs to the roof.

I'd never been so high in my life. From this perspective it was as if we'd expanded and Lumena Hills was in miniature. The roof was full though I didn't recognize anyone. They didn't seem much older than us though they looked sophisticated in some way, maybe it was their slender figures and sheer clothes in dark hues—friends of Jeni's, I assumed. Someone had toted up boxes of old printed books, novels and poetry collections with pages folded. We took turns standing on the roof's ledge, shouting words from the musty pages, spitting them into the night.

Jeni gave us each two more Delixir. I felt I could step off the ledge and float across the night. Jeni asked if we'd heard anything more about Celia. Azzie nodded, "She's going to be fine." I liked the sound of this, it was noddingly good news, fine finisimo yes, and so I nodded back at her, and we just sat back and fell into each other.

Jeni told us that the Lady Lupine Moon was the largest of the year as we lay on our backs and looked up at its glow in the pit of the sky. Or that's what it looked like at first—I soon realized that it was still overcast. This moon was just a projection.

"What does the lupine part mean?" I asked her.

Jeni said that it was guarded by the spirit of the wolf and that under its light we would retreat into our animal natures. The moon's blood would fall to earth as if it were menstruating and when it did we'd be revitalized.

"Just look at that redness," Azzie said. "I feel it entering me." She turned and licked Jeni's shoulder.

"And when it falls through the atmosphere we'll

spontaneously combust," Jeni said back to her.

"And have simultaneous orgasms!"

"You're both full of it," I laughed.

The moon was deep red, like the shade of maple trees in fall just as their leaves die. I was filled with desire, for them, for all of this ripening. Jeni passed a rabbit pelt to me. I rubbed it on my cheek and thought how it too was once a living thing. I passed it to Azzie. She said she could feel its spirit with us now, swore she saw its presence hovering just above the flood lamp. And for a moment all was quiet at twenty stories high.

Jeni gave us a ride back to Azzie's, gave her a big kiss and shoved us out. We went to the back of the house and climbed on her trampoline. There we split the last tab of Delixir and downed it with an Edge Eraser. I lay down and Azzie started jumping, making my body bounce. I pulled her legs and she fell over me and wouldn't move and I started pushing her off. She grabbed my hands and soon we slipped to the ground. We flipped over each other and stumbled down a narrow path. She pulled out more pills and I opened my mouth. She broke a capsule over my tongue, and then placed her mouth on mine.

We swung suspended. I wanted to drink her warmth.

She ran from me, down to the river. I followed her, as the first of morning light crept into the sky. We walked out over the river on the wooden dock. She got down on her stomach, ran her hands through the water. "Let's get in," she said, and we stripped off our clothes and jumped. The water was waist-deep and freezing. We ran through the water shivering, and just as quickly jumped out again. I lay down, then Azzie lay beside me. We watched the sky as it started to brighten.

Next thing I knew I woke beside Azzie, her hot breath on my back. Even my skin felt weary. I took all of my energy to focus on the chair in the distance. I felt like I could hardly catch my breath. It took so much to think, *roll out of bed*, before my body responded. And Celia—the thought of her landed. I felt so out of sync with the night before. I wanted to slip back into the pleasure.

I got up and showered to wash away the weight in my chest. When I came back Azzie was still in bed, though half awake. I sat beside her and asked if Trinie had sent any more messages.

She shook her head no and looked confused.

"... last night you said she'd said Celia was fine."

"I didn't say that I'd heard anything. Trinie was busy, her nights always are. But Celia's fine, I'm sure."

"But she's not, obvi. She hasn't texted us or anything. Azzie, can't you take anything seriously?"

"Chill, Hannah. Really, what could we have done last night anyway?"

"I just don't think it's right to let our guard down, to feel so light when like, our friend is in trouble."

"So it's not enough for Celia to be distraught. You've got to add to the mix."

I was so frustrated, I'm not sure who with more, Azzie or myself, but I didn't have energy for it. "That's not it. It's just whatever's happening with her is serious."

"Like your dead animals list."

"Too bad the night had to end this way." I pulled on my dress without much acknowledgement and mumbled about needing to get air.

Azzie called out after me, "It was a delight."

When I got home Judy was perched by the door. She looked down at her watch, then back at me as if she wanted me to respond. She swallowed her hello in a way that told me I'd been out too long, missed my doses, but she wasn't going to say anything more. She followed me into the kitchen, where I found the cups of pills—four side by side. She'd left them out, as if a way to measure time. I downed all four at once right there in front of her face so she'd stop watching.

I spent the afternoon going over my lessons, but no use. Words, ideas, clips just slid through my mind. Later I went up to the observatory and lay down on the warm floor. I closed my eyes and just tried to breathe and as soon as I did, I felt my device vibrate.

Azzie. "C's been admitted to psych. They're keeping her for observation."

My heart sank. "I wouldn't call that *FINE*."

"I know, H. She was in a way. Trinie's following the situation."

I paused to consider. Azzie's mother and her updates were as good as we'd get. Proximity, good conscience, holding her in our mind, wouldn't change anything. It didn't keep species from dying. It wouldn't help Celia now. Celia's mother likely would burn incense and light candles, form a sacred chanting circle to create vibrations. But for whom. It's not like holding Celia in mind would help stabilize her, send her home. Still, I wanted to do something. I soon realized I was too spent to wrestle with this, with thoughts of Azzie, and my discontents.

I wished that I could be oblivious to it and re-enter the bliss of the night before. How distant its pleasure seemed, though also so close, almost as if I could feel the energetic traces on my lips, in my fingers. I yearned for more.

DELIXIR is available in 25mg, 50mg, and 100mg tablets and 37.5mg oral disintegrating wafers. Place the wafer under the tongue to dissolve The dose may be titrated up until a full therapeutic effect is achieved.

XI

At dinner the next evening Judy walked from kitchen to table, from table to kitchen, paused, and circled again. Took sharp steps in smart pencil leg pants, her hair swept up in a bun, foundation without flaw, lists piled by her plate.

"Flash-cooked greens with amino acid flakes ready in three minutes or less. While we're waiting, why don't you tell us what you've reviewed today?"

Harold nodded to the cadence of her voice.

I sat silent and she glared.

Harold offered: "New telescopes are in place. Images are returning, peculiar craters on a distant moon. Possible presence of water, possible signs of life. No breaks to be taken until analysis is complete."

"I wasn't asking *you*." Judy sighed as he forked his meat.

Judy sat down and took the tiniest bite of beans, sipped a fizzy drink. "Well, let me start. I have an efficiency appointment with Susan. Toast and Roasters tomorrow, 10am. Should be a cinch."

She had me prepare a daily list of what happened under headings: Occurrences, Emotions, Tasks Completed, Obstacles Overcome, Pills Taken, Lessons Reviewed, What Is vs. What Will Be. I resented schedule-talk. Judy knew how much I hated this recitation.

She marked her list with a strong flick of the wrist. Harold sat scratching his ear, then muttered something about metals that could withstand the heat of re-entering the atmosphere.

He looked at me, said he wished he'd recorded more when he was my age. "V. didn't exist, memory wasn't as deep." When he was young he'd wanted to travel to distant galaxies. Harness the energy of stars. "Imagine... the advances I could've made...."

This I noted. Harold wanted to relive his youth.

Judy asked about Celia, said she'd heard something about her being in the hospital. Was it true?

I shrugged.

"Oh dear!" Harold sighed.

Judy nodded, said how terrible, whispered something about *fragility*. But she spoke around it just like everything. I went back to sketching the slump of Harold's shoulders on my napkin, then the outline of Judy's pursed lips. I tried to visualize the waves of information moving through us in that instant.

I offered that I'd made another death mask last week. I showed them the image with yellow almonds for eyes, cheeks like cliffs to jump from.

"Oh Hannah, why?"

"I did another quick scan of Azzie's face. Each one ends up so different, depending on her mood." I told her how I planned to catalog all of my friends. I couldn't predict the varied ways the gloves picked up the contours, the rise of her cheekbones, the depths of her eyes.

"Isn't Azulea very much alive?"

"That's not the point. Death mask as in it's a readymade relic for our pre-instinctual phase. Before the transformation of our lives into another state." Ultimately, I planned to 3D print the most striking faces and hang them.

"Yes," Harold nodded, "Currently in mid-Sixth. Oceans warming, scorched trees, carbon dated."

Harold had always said we were mid-Sixth, as in a period of great extinction. He liked to tell me that this made things exciting, like it was opening the door for the possibility of some other life form to take over. But I couldn't get past how this meant we had no future.

The future Judy spoke of seemed like a lie. She thought we should all do our best to try to be content. Happy, joyous even. I didn't know how she could ignore that we were in the middle of the Sixth and waiting for the worst.

Judy paused and made notes. I'm sure it was something like: *Death Mask. Conflicted. Uneven distribution of energy.*

"Happiness" was Judy's baseline, against which she pitted all other moods. Negativity had to be contained. She had a whole spiel about happiness as a determined state.

She got up and threw the leftover greens into the compost, placed dishes on autoclave, and then set out my organizer and pills for the next day. She added ones I hadn't seen before: spheres in blue hues, lemon-yellow triangles. Then she gave me a handful of spheres and triangles and a glass of water.

They felt sharp in my palms.

"Take two and chew well."

"But what do they do?"

"They'll help stabilize your moods."

After dinner Judy made us watch a video. She was adding video programming to her practice, in a collaboration with Dr. Billy. He was curating a regimen of enhancements to complement Judy's four-step program.

"Four is a cinch to implement," she says in the promotional video. "Four steps, four enhancements, four times a day. Four is all you have to remember."

Personal responsibility was something else she stressed. She's standing in front of the factory gardens and says: "You are responsible for your own sink or swim,"—just like she always told her clients. "Take control of your life in four simple steps: Seed, Sprout, Root, Grow."

It worked so well for her somehow. Judy's clients

were promised results within four meetings. She'd helped many a weary neighbor structure enhancement schedules for their children. "You'd never guess how many mix it up, miss doses, and don't consider how detrimental this is."

She said I was lucky to have her undivided attention. But I knew her secrets. Like she couldn't function without consulting a flow chart first.

"No such thing as perfection but why not try! Seeds too crowded, too scattered? You reap what you sow."

When the video ended Judy asked what I thought. I replied that it seemed exactly like she'd described. She took this as positive, then grabbed my hand. "I have a surprise!"

She shared her screen and scrolled through images of a series of women lying in loungers clustered together, each in identical white pantsuits, holding conch shells in their hands. The spa's 'miracle mud' was harvested from local caverns, and all communicative transmissions were blocked by surrounding rock formations. And—despite its location beyond Lumena's limits, the spa complied with standards of communication and surveillance.

"A device-free weekend for inward focus and bonding," Judy exclaimed.

I dreaded the idea of an entire weekend with Judy without my devices. It would stretch for an eternity.

She would spend it tipping scales, calibrating and titrating and navel gazing—and what would I do in the absence of streams?

Judy insisted the weekend would be good for me. For us. She said she'd planned a nip and tuck, lift and suck, dermal rejuvenation for herself. For both of us: morning salutations with Chatterlock and Mental Floss. Also, a full course of SweatNSwirl (*The Workout in a Pill*)™ and a sensory deprivation tank augmented by XTRA_lyfe.

At least it sounded like she'd spend most of her time having cosmetic work done.

"There's nothing worse than mother-daughter disconnect," she said, looking at me tenderly. She was somehow trying to close our distance but I wished I wasn't the one who had to make up for it. Judy tried to command me as if this were a form of love. Maybe it was.

Spas were her thing, not mine. She knew this. Still. She said we'd go the following weekend, and we'd make do.

THE TEDIUM OF ONE SO WHY NOT TWO
A CAT HAS NINE—DON'T YOU DESERVE MORE TOO?

XTRA_lyfe is your plus one when life turns lackluster and you're just going through the motions.

Take XTRA-lyfe to revive.

XII.

A luxury shuttle picked us up just outside our home and we were offered preliminary detox tonics en route. The compound was located just south of town. On our way, we passed by a series of houses growing smaller and warehouses growing larger, and endless rows of grand silos that I assumed were storage for the factory's raw materials. This industrial sector continued for a while and then we crossed a bridge over a rock formation and followed a long winding road that went deeper into a valley. I wondered what creatures were lurking out here. I attempted to imagine the wildness we were bypassing, what lay just beyond, the lizards and beetles and coyotes and foxes and feral cats. This was as close as I'd come to the wilderness. And yet somehow we were safe all the way out here at *Spa L'Cran Noir*, rock fortress and all.

Our suite was on the third floor; it had large windows and was fitted with counters cut from obsidian and its cabinets were stocked with powders and empty capsules. "All natural," Judy said.

The room held two king-sized beds equipped with netting to equalize emotional forces. It came with two no-breathe bodysuits, two suits with loose-cut legs, and a stack of clean bathrobes in the bathroom closet.

Judy undressed. I pretended not to look at her delicate body. I wondered how she'd ever had room for me inside of her and how much she'd hated the engorgement. She still had stretch marks on her thighs.

She put on her robe, knotted her belt, and examined the jars of black dust on the counter. "Have I mentioned obsidian's healing properties?"

Many times. She loved explaining this and so I said, "I don't think so?"

"Well, dear, this stone has a strong protective shield that absorbs negative energy waves. It's very healing. We'll have to do something with it!"

Judy tucked our cases in the closets, placed our vials and jars on shelves and in empty drawers while I began my own count of what the cabinets held. They were stocked with 'natural' products—jars of wondrous colored dust: crushed crystal, amethyst, obsidian, iso-dehydrated sage and garlic, and turmeric concentrate. The bottom of each glass had an "L" stamped upon it. They were made and bottled by Lumena too, I assumed. I'd heard Lumea made a line of high-end products that harnessed ancient energetic forces from our forests and deserts; some were natural equivalents, though some were imported. It seemed odd to me, considering how the forest, or really any resource beyond our township was off limits for common use.

Judy made an energy drink from a powder and our

tap of purified spring water. I went out on the balcony and was impressed by the rocks and sand, and what looked like old-school satellite dishes. It resembled what I imagined a desert would look like IRL, and whatever, it was much more exotic than Lumena Hills.

Judy soon joined me outdoors. She said she hadn't ever heard such silence. Away from the whir of the factory, no generators, no vehicles. She looked out and took in the view and commented on the incredible specimen of nature before us. I settled into the hammock with my device in case they were lying about no reception. Then I pulled the netting around me.

Judy smiled, "I see you're acclimating."

"Not so fast," I said.

"Oh of course—you're not." She knew I wouldn't admit to having a modicum of pleasure.

I turned on my device. It searched and searched for the wifi stream but the revolving circle just spun like a hastening hurricane.

"Signal's dead," I pouted.

"Of course it is. But just wait. After the extraction, post-cleanse, you'll feel like a new person."

"I imagine I'll feel exactly like the person I am."

"No judgments, Hannah? Besides, we have an entire evening for the initial unwinding. It says right here." She passed me a card that listed the master schedule and various services. It reminded me of her 4-Step Method with its simple bullet point lists. Perhaps she'd intended to glean some pointers for her marketing plan while we were out here.

"Well let's not waste the evening!" she exclaimed. "I'd like to go to the jacuzzi or the steam baths, your pick. First, though, we could mix some obsidian and clay facials?"

I agreed to the facial and said I'd decide later about the rest. I took off what the spa called my *day clothes* and put on a robe. I mixed the clay with spring water in a bowl and added two scoops of obsidian. I then rubbed mixture on Judy's face, as she lay reclined. It was soothing to cover her face with dark mud. Is it wrong to say I enjoyed feeling like I was desecrating her? Because I did. I felt her delicate cheekbones and her tensed expression below my fingers, as she struggled to hold her eyes closed. She laughed and said, "It's so hard for me to let go!"

I painted my own face with the dark mud, assessing myself in the mirror as I slathered it on. I imagined I was a warrior. I'd seen my chimp family bathing in mud puddles massive enough to take all fifteen at once. It pleased me that in our own way we were behaving very much like chimps.

I set a timer and sat back next to Judy. We were silent for a while and then she asked, "How are you processing?" She didn't say "Celia." She definitely didn't mention Ms. Tigue.

"I'm fine I guess?" I said I didn't really know how to measure it, but I was worried for my friend.

"Don't worry your pretty head. She's being taken care of. You know, her family might not want everyone knowing their business."

"But what if it's because of, you know, her V.—? She's an over-reactor like me. Aren't you concerned?"

"Honey, I believe in you, and I trust in Dr. Billy and Lumena, their testing and monitoring."

I washed my face off with a sponge and it looked like it was bleeding. The sponge was shaped like a weird-ass polygon.

Judy said the sponge was "real."

"Like it was living once?"

She nodded. It kind of blew my mind. I made note to look this up when we had reception again.

Judy went on to the jacuzzi but I stayed in the room and turned off the lights. From my bed I could stare up through the skylight into the night. For a while I just lay there in awe of the darkness.

The next morning I woke to a seismic bed shake and the sound of Judy's imperative voice: "Ten minutes until your 11am!"

"Okay, okay," I muttered, and sat up. When I opened my eyes there was no sign of Judy, just the dark obsidian counters and my pill case set out next to a glass of water. I pulled on a robe and opened the blinds.

I'd missed the sunrise meditation.

I swallowed the capsules Judy had laid out before I pulled on a bodysuit and exited. Despite the lack of streams I had the uncanny sense that someone was watching me.

The lobby's shimmer resembled the inside of a large clam. It opened to a series of tunnels, some rising into glass walkways. A sign indicated that pools and hot springs and landscape views were available along the Upper Loop. The other tunnels led down, burrowed into the thermal pits, the meditation chambers and deprivation chambers and mud coves, which I was particularly interested in. Everything hot and dirty was down there.

Hazel, my spa therapist, was waiting for me at the lobby desk. She glowed.

"You're sparkly," I said. She looked kind of sweaty, actually.

"Effervescent," she corrected. This, she said, would be included in my spa treatment. "Your exterior will soon exude your inner clarity."

"I can't wait."

"Oh you don't even know how invigorating this will be."

My sarcasm didn't even make her pause. She asked me if I'd like to know my treatment schedule. I declined.

"You like surprises," she noted. "Okay, well let's

get on with it!" She led me on an upward trail and pointed out the large rock formations, emphasizing they were *truly* natural. She explained that they had been excavated from some faraway desert.

From there she led me into an alcove that led to a stone proscenium open to air. At its center was one of the satellite dishes, inverted and filled with water.

"The cooling pool," she said. "It draws positive energies from the outer atmosphere. Perhaps even beyond. This is your first session. Duration, one hour."

I could handle that. There was snow beyond us but my perch was warm.

Hazel placed a plate of gelatin cubes beside me and told me to start eating. I consumed a few. They tasted buoyant and minerally. Soon I felt warmer.

She came back and leaned over. "Oh honey, don't deprive yourself," she urged and then waited for me to consume the entire plate. She placed a thermometer on my chest and told me to disrobe, submerge entirely, then come up for air.

She warned: "It may not feel pleasant at first."

I jumped in and just as quickly regretted it. Toes burning, chest on fire. "What the monkey hell!" I yelled. "I'd rather walk on hot coals."

Hazel came over and acknowledged the paradoxical effect: "The cold will make you feel like you're burning, yes?"

"I want out!" She stood there watching as I squirmed until I felt the abhorrent heat passing.

Hazel lifted me out and placed me on the mat. I couldn't feel my body. She pushed her fingers into my back and thighs and all I could feel was slight pressure. She wrapped me in a net and turned on a heat lamp.

"Hazel?! Let me go and I won't tell a soul."

She smiled vacantly. Her skin was brilliant and cruel. "Exterior reflects inner glow. Judging by your baseline you're due for extraction."

"Not so!"

She tsk-tsk'd me. "Too clogged. It will take a while to dissolve."

I wanted to vomit dark bile all over. Instead, I retched pitifully into the pan beside me. Hazel unwrapped me and left me under the lamp. I fell asleep until she came back and woke me.

"Next up! Thermal coves!" She was as spritely as before. I'd wanted to witness this mud bath, it was perhaps the only thing I wanted to do here.

"I will go but under the condition of no more torture," I said.

"No pain no gain!" she said, then laughed. "Well, that's not always true. But this treatment should be more amenable to you."

Hazel led me back through the upper tunnels and we came to an entryway to the underground.

We descended into the caves, which looked like the beginning of a maze. "What's down here?" I asked, and she listed all the hot and horrid treatments: mud baths, rock and crystal saunas, deprivation chambers, salt baths, heat treatment. I imagined we were literally walking down into the inner core of the earth, where I was sure I'd be subjected to another version of hell. If this were so, I hoped there'd be a tar pit for flatterers too.

We passed doors whose deep red hue made them camouflage with the wall.

"And that?" I asked.

"Oh, you know, the entrance to the underworld. Dressing rooms, meeting rooms, environmental services HQ."

I nodded as if I knew what this meant. We stopped at the entrance to an expansive underground cave, with a hard rock floor and rows of baths filled with mud. Alcoves lined both sides of the cave.

"Voilà—the mud baths! Let me get one started for you." She led me to a pool and pressed a button beside it. The mud started to churn. "Disrobe again, dear."

I frowned.

"This one will be more soothing for your dominant bilious side. I promise."

I undressed and got in. What she'd said was true. I felt like I was swimming in a thick cup of hot chocolate. It smelled spiced. She said that when the jets stopped I was to get out and enter one of the alcoves emitting a red glow. Inside I'd find an eye pillow. I was to lay on the mat. Then she'd come back.

Hazel couldn't take the heat, she said. Her skin looked a bit splotchy down here. She assured me she'd be back in time for my next treatment.

I squeezed the warm mud between my fingers and toes. I enjoyed it even more knowing Judy wasn't watching my every move. I heard a small group of women walk past as I floated. When the jets turned off I did as instructed, found a cave and a mat. I lay down for a while, the clay baking onto my skin, but eventually it dried and felt itchy.

I decided to see if I could find a shower. I put on a robe and went back into the main cave. I found a towel stand but no showers. I asked the towel attendant where they were. He said I had to wait for my therapist to return.

I frowned. "How long?"

"Depends" he said, "who are you assigned to?"

"Hazel?"

He looked at his watch, swiped it. Said I had twenty minutes.

"That's an eternity!"

He laughed. He didn't look much older than me. He was what I thought other women would deem attractive. He had a lean muscular physique, pale freckled skin, blonde hair. His name tag had the name Äsa. This Äsa was very hygge-worthy, but did nothing for me. I wasn't often attracted to anyone it seemed, and when I was they were usually dark and inattentive to their musculature. I lamented not being able to even use him for a towel boy fantasy. He did however concede to give me a short tour of the secret underworld here. We walked through a door that was camouflaged into the wall, and it led to a nondescript stairwell with rails and EXIT signs just like an office building. We went down a few flights until we reached level B#3, where we exited to a long hall lined with large pipes and walked quickly through a series of locker rooms, a staff cafeteria and dispensary, break rooms for naps and overnights, and a large laundry facility. It was dizzying. I asked if he ever felt claustrophobic down here, like the ground would fall in upon him?

He shook his head and eyed me like this was a crazy suggestion. "You need this extraction, don't you." He led me into a room whose four walls were active screens. Each screen was broken into multiple individual feeds.

"So there *is* a wifi connection. But why the fuck do you spy on people?"

He said it wasn't like that. "Of course we have wifi. And no one really watches the feeds. They're mostly just accessible for patron requests." The 'patrons,' as he called us, like to share memories. Some wanted access for wellness documentation, life logs, or whatever. "It's far easier for the patron to remain present if they know they can recapture the moment without having to record it."

"Does everyone know this?"

He nodded.

"Then my mother must too." Not about this room specifically but that she could watch what I did and see how I performed. I felt so exposed knowing that my movements were surveilled here, if not witnessed at the least recorded. I hoped that if Judy watched my replays, she would see the torture of my extraction.

The towel boy said that of course she knew—she had to sign a waiver, everyone did. The waiver included a list of what she could access and allowed her to request the documentation she'd have access to when we left.

WTF, not surprising. Knowing this made me feel a bit salty. I asked if any of the women hired towel boys like him to walk on their backs.

He smirked.

"Well?"

"It's not like you're thinking."

"... okay, so?!"

He said there were no orgies but yes, they offered an array of sexual healing practices. These were available only to patrons of a certain age. I wondered if Judy had enrolled in any of those.

"It's very professional. You know, massages, doses of AutoRox, our tailored packages, immersion in our pheromone emitting tonic. In the Rox massage they're used in succession, though sometimes together."

I said I did want a massage—camera off—but not the rest, was that possible?

Äsa touched my back and asked if he could assess my level of contraction. His hands hovered over my shoulders, down my spine, and assessed the contours.

"Feels like a slab of granite." He seemed very assured of his competence. Also, I couldn't tell if he was making a joke of it.

"Oh also, can you, I mean I'd love some AutoRox?" I eyed him, "You know, *discreetly*."

"I'll see what I can do." He swiped his device. "Hm.... I can slip you in before your eight o'clock. Might be a little tight, but yes?"

I agreed, and we walked back and up the stairs and through the door just in time to meet Hazel.

"Hannah!" she effused. "How does that mud feel?"

"A bit itchy."

"Well, you look like a million dollars. I told you this procedure would do you some good."

"Eh no need to exaggerate," I said. "What I really need is a good wash."

She sent me off to the shower and to lunch with Judy, then I returned to the room where I passed the rest of the afternoon in a cleanse and chelation. I could've gone to yet another treatment room for this but I chose to stay close to my own bathroom for the eruptions that often accompanied this treatment. When I wasn't surrendering to the toilet I was sitting on the balcony outside feeling woozy. Though at moments, on the lounger with the net surrounding me, I'd dare to say it almost felt peaceful.

Later, toward evening, I heard a knock on the door. An attendant in white handed me a bag—a sackful of tiny pink crystals. The attendant directed me to take one now, and another in twenty minutes, and then to show up with my robe at the entrance to the inner dunes at 7pm. Äsa had come through.

I took one rock and nothing. Nothing after I took the second either. This was a bit of a disappointment, but not more so than the rest of the spa trip so far. And so I set out, through the inner clam to the Upper Loop and the dune room. I'd never experienced dunes IRL, like so many natural formations, and I was curious to see this replication. I'd mostly read about them because of the dune lizard, who was a longtime member on the endangered list. This lizard lived in real dunes, though, not like this, and in blowouts, which to me sounded like magnificent parties but really were the pockets and crevices in the sand sculpted by wind. I knew I'd find nothing so exotic or alive, no such animals or crevices here.

I was given a pair of slip-on paper booties and a slim-fit bodysuit to change into before I was admitted to the black sands room. *L'cran noir*, namesake of this spa, I was told by a pale woman wearing all black who looked rather bored and spoke to me as if I was too young to know anything. She led me to an anteroom with positive pressure. The door slid open just enough for me to walk through and closed quickly behind me. I wandered through a series of rooms filled with sand drifts. I was completely alone. I wondered if this too was part of the curated experience.

I made my way through the rooms to the outside. When I stepped out I stood atop the highest in a series of dunes. There was a pool at the base. The sun had just set and we were at the tail end of the gloaming. I sat down, with my back to the wall and I watched the silhouettes of the compound, its outdoor assortment of craggy rocks, the hills further in the distance, as all fell from deep purple into darkness. How odd to not be able to see the factory from here. Somehow I felt bereft and enticed. This thought soon faded, though, as the pleasure within me bloomed. It was as if my skin had just molted. Even the hint of wind gave me chills. I removed my booties, slid my feet into the sand, and I closed my eyes to take it in.

I must've lost track of time. I was surprised when I heard the rustle of someone behind me, then Äsa apologizing. "Sorry, I was double booked. Though we still have time for a quickie. I heard your package was delivered?"

Did he say hard? Or was it his dialect which seemed a bit of a variant, just like that umlaut over the A on his nametag? I was preoccupied with this, these sounds that vibrated within me. I just nodded and hummed an mmmhmmm. His presence was far more disarming than I recalled from earlier in the day. He was wearing a black t-shirt and I didn't really care what came out of his hygge mouth because when he touched me it was pure delight.

"I see you took your Rox. Good, good."

He lay a sheet on the sand and had me lie face-down on a donut-shaped pillow. He then placed a sheet over me and started to pound my back with his fists.

"Oh, oh my!" I wriggled with surprise.

"Too hard?"

That word again. "No, no, just right. The pleasure into pain, I've never felt it quite like this."

"Just let go," he said, "I'll do the rest."

"Do I get a happy ending? I don't want a disappointing one."

He didn't answer, he just slathered oil on my back and it flowed down my sides. This was really too much for me and if I hadn't been so lost in my delight I would've had the mind to push him off me.

"Mmmm more of that," was all I could utter, as

his hands flew over my ass, and started massaging my thighs. He named the muscles as he touched them, "adductor," "vast crest," and something that sounded like "semi-tendentious." They all sounded so delicious, I just hmmmmmed my way through it, and then he opened my right hand that lay by my side and placed a stone in my palm.

"I'm done," he announced. "No need to get up until you're ready—or until the notice for your next appointment plays. You'll make your way down the dune, through the wading pool to the shower. You can orchestrate your own finale."

"Like a choose your own adventure?"

"If that's what pleases you."

"Äsaaaa." I moaned. "I hate so much about this place but you are the beeest." He walked off and I lay there for what seemed like a second until I heard an announcement that my session had ended. I walked down the dune—the air I breathed had never felt so fresh—and through the pool, still surprisingly warm, to the shower. The lights were dim, and the water fell in a soft and tepid stream. I looked at the rock in my hand. I ran my fingers over it. This was pleasing. Then I squeezed it, and the rock started to vibrate. Ah! I realized what Äsa had meant by my own adventure. The voice overhead started berating me for my lateness and so I stuck the rock in my robe pocket for later, at home, with the rest of my Rox.

At my 8pm, they had me climb into a white plastic container that looked like a cross between a trashcan and an egg. I was told there was a supplement in the water that would aid in loosening awareness of the outside world.

I dove headfirst into the liquid and they shut the lid. I had been told this would clear my head, that the lack of sensation would amplify what stewed within and needed release, and to do this I should focus only on physical sensations. I had the sense of being ferried across a river and thrown into this putrid swimhole. I was overcome by angst and tenderness and so many impressions and feelings apparently built up within me. I could barely breathe and then vomited. This set off an alarm and soon they pulled me out and placed me in the shower.

Apparently the Rox's heightened state of sensation was a contraindication and shouldn't have been followed by sensory deprivation, which induced visions and pain along with a general sense of listlessness that lasted for days. I was exhausted and stumbled into bed afterward, and I barely made it to brunch the next day. I was permitted to skip my remaining sessions for poolside recovery, where I sat under a heat lamp and was served a constant stream of e-lyte+ water. "The better for flushing," Hazel said. She again was waiting on me.

On the ride back to Lumena Hills that evening, I

107

stared out into the darkness. Judy was uncharacteristically quiet, perhaps she was exhausted too. Or maybe she'd taken a parting dose of Chatterlock. I was grateful for the silence and to look out into the dark night into the vastness that lay beyond.

After we returned home, I found Judy's account of the trip on the table, alongside my meds. Was it intentional? Who knows. Of course I read it:

SPA WEEKEND!

SAT
11am. Hmmm. Mhmmm.
2pm. Words return. Smoothly, without awkward halt, pause or stutter.
Time for mental floss in an obsidian chamber.
5pm. H called hyperthermic treatment "torture," tanks "wicked."
Wicked = good, sometimes? Not sure.
Hyperthermic treatment detox not pleasant when buildup is present.
Mood (mine): sour, obsidian stirs up sediment; breaks down recalcitrant layers.
Will try to remedy with chelating cleanse & liquid chasers.
8pm. Crow's feet extracted, spider veins covered, shar pei skin now taut.

H's evening: zero gravity isolation chamber. Reduction recharges.

12am. Hannah returned with hallucinations. Nausea, excess bile.

Next time, if there is, a salt float is advised.

SUN

12pm. Oh, tired aches, oh cricks and cracks, oh sun swelter, oh charley horse hamstring, oh oh ouch. I've taken a beating with SweatNSwirl. On to the meditation cave, epiphany in a pill?! Followed by XTRA _lyfe release.

H: Gourmand's breakfast: pancakes, syrup, sausage and eggs, platters of donuts and bagels and lox and a schmear; hash browns, waldorf salad, eggs benedict with hollandaise and bacon. all concocted with calories extracted? Must inquire how to order at home.

5pm. Apparently H is still bilious from excess. Two days is too few for total extraction.

Trying to ignore.

Would be a pity for H's irritability to tarnish my memories of this trip.

Judy noted the weekend as "failure to take root." She called me resentful.

I found a note along with this. It was addressed to Dr. Billy, asking him to increase my doses. She said she agreed with his assessment. She wanted to make me more tractable, she said.

I felt betrayed.

I scrawled a note back on her tablet: "Fuck that— love, my inner fucking cat."

"That's exactly what I'm talking about," Judy spat at me the next morning. "Your hostility. There are pills for this."

Dr. Billy would take care of it. She said she had made an appointment. A mother had to make sure. She was rooting for me, didn't I see?

*¡¡**<u>AUTOROX</u>** WILL KNOCK YOUR SOCKS OFF!!*

XIII.

So much hush-hush going round made the silence of Celia's absence so loud. No one knew what had happened for sure. Speculation was Celia had taken the wrong pills in the wrong way, or too many at the wrong time, or possibly she'd never had enough. The inverse function of EmptEZ may have jumbled her brain waves, or the doubling up deranged her foundations.

Dr. Billy issued a school-wide notice: *Remember to take ONLY AS DIRECTED. Some supplements must be stopped before others are begun. Doubling up doesn't mean doubling the effect. Sometimes one supplement must be stopped before another is started. Sometimes one must be accompanied by another. Sometimes misuse is harmless and others, it's catastrophic.* The memo didn't mention Celia by name but I knew it was about her, quite obvi.

Everything seemed fragmented but oddly this drew us together, like our previous table regrouped for midday dosing. Samuel and Linnaeus, however, now refused to make trades. Doreen told us that Celia's mother had asked for prayers and healing energies, and since Celia left I had no one to give me afternoon relief with their Sunkisses. Doreen also reported that Samsun's table now talked about how Azzie and I were also deranged. Samsun called our confrontation "bizarre" and said that it was an ill-conceived over-reaction to Celia's unrequited feelings. The fuckers. We decided to send Samsun the evil eye for Celia's sake when we saw him. I imagined sending darts of toad poison with my line of vision every time.

Azzie agreed to meet me daily before classes to send Celia good karma in the off chance that this might actually help her. Besides, we knew it would make her happy if she knew we were doing this. The first day we met it was colder out, and we could see our breath rise as if the energies we were sending were materializing. Azzie said they should be good energies, like whiffs of Insta_Pleasure. I said we should add Celia to the endangered list too. Azzie agreed, though I also wondered if Azzie thought I was again taking things too seriously. There was a distance between us that seemed to extend from the closeness of that night and our fight. Like Azzie seemed more guarded talking about her crushes. Or maybe I just didn't want to hear about them. The only things we knew with any certainty about Celia were relayed through Trinie. Like, Celia was still in psych. And that she'd been stabilized, but that didn't mean anything other than she wasn't getting worse. Celia's mother visited her often, though all she did was sit in the corner reciting mantras on her mala beads. Her father, apparently, hadn't stepped foot in the hospital. It all seemed so sad and dire.

Celia's mother would have to approve our visitation and she wouldn't return our calls. Maybe because she had no good news to share—or she didn't want us to see Celia in her current state. Azzie said she probably just had other things on her mind.

"But why does no one talk about it, mention Celia's condition?"

"Maybe so we don't worry. We're still acclimating, you know?"

To send energies we closed our eyes, inhaled and exhaled slowly for a minute thinking of sending warmth to Celia. I thought of the warm energy as a sparrow at her window. I thought of the energy moving invisibly from Lumena High across town to the hospital and Celia bathing in it. It seemed impossible and yet, I knew the air was filled with information, seemingly infinite amounts of it washed over us every second. If that was the case then surely it was possible that we could send energy to Celia, even if she wasn't aware of it.

The following week I received an S.O.S. It arrived in a padded envelope with a small piece of paper folded into a square. Celia's lines were shaky, as if she stuttered as she wrote. The message, when summarized, was bland. Nice meals, fine people, will be home soon. No mention of what was wrong with her, no anger, no sadness. The weeks on the ward had blanched her. Or the stabilizers had flattened her too.

I crumpled the envelope but felt a thickness in the middle. I looked again. I found a small piece of cardboard inserted within. The cardboard was covered in writing. I had to use a magnifying glass to decipher it:

Oh my fucking buddha I hope you get this. Need your help. Talk of erasure therapy, the one and only dr. billy. Blames ME. I'm 'volatile' apparently took too much EmptEZ, a no-no with Insta_Pleasure or anger or too much emotional outpouring. Mother here every so often, nothing more dreary. Sits in a corner and cries. I'm doing better than her, I swear. Just sad. Sometimes so sad I don't move. I mean, what can I do? Can't stand it here, can't stand the meds. They've started infusions. Want to rip them out. Go cold turkey. Dead turkey? Gobble gobble my brains out. If I die in here, burn me on a pyre.

I didn't know how to help her. I messaged Azzie to let her know. *Can we meet?*

She responded: *YES. TONIGHT?*

Apparently, she'd gotten a message too.

Azzie showed up at the back door late looking rather ragged, her hair tied up in a kerchief. She followed me downstairs. She took the couch and I sat across from her on the ottoman. Even though I saw her daily at school, since that night we hadn't spent much time alone together. We were just the same as before, except there was so much of this muchness between us. She held up a scrolled paper that Celia had given to her mother to give to her—Trinie had been able to visit during her shift the night before. Celia had told Trinie she'd been so lonely, that even her mother hadn't visited in days.

Azzie unrolled the paper. It was a watercolor of Factory Hill obscured mostly by smoke.

"Must be her view?"

"But wait, look." The back of the watercolor had a second, smaller piece of paper attached. Azzie unfolded it, then laid it on the floor. It revealed the floor plan for the psych wing, with one floor in detail, the children's unit on the 3rd floor.

Celia had drawn an X to mark her bed and room, with double lines for windows and angled lines for doors. The communal rooms were demarcated by animals: a crane, a crocodile, and a bear. It was possible the bear was a badger?

She had drawn a key to the map at the bottom, along with a list of patient names and room numbers and diagnoses. I didn't know any of them well, but I knew many of the names.

"I have no idea what she means by this," I said.

"The animals, are they nurses? Who do you think

she likes better, the crane or the crocodile?"

"My money's on the bear, the badger, whatever. This is absurd."

I looked at the diagram for a while. It occurred to me that these were all animals George Gordon Byron had kept in his menagerie when he lived in Switzerland with the Shelleys. But would Celia have known this? Byron loved and lived with animals. I'd been infatuated with him for a time. But even so I didn't know what these animals represented. I mean, the whooping crane was extinct and many other species were endangered. It was just as likely that rooms on the children's ward had animal themes. *Something cutesy, less intimidating*, I could hear Judy saying.

"Do you think we can help her get out?" I asked.

"I don't see how we have any say in it."

"Well, your mother could get us in."

"And then?"

" I don't know. We'd have to figure it out."

Azzie shrugged and looked at me like I was crazy. Said her mother probably could get us in if we wanted. Trinie had also told her that Celia's case was complex. With so many fissures and fault lines in her mind, she was more fragile than she appeared.

I handed Azzie the message on cardboard I'd received.

"What's this?"

"Use your device's magnifier and read."

She scrunched her eyes and read and as she did I tried to think about why Celia had sent this. It was clear that she wasn't just a vegetable, this was good. It also seemed that she was panicked.

"Erasure therapy?!" Azzie exclaimed.

"Talk of it—" I hadn't really considered that 'talk' meant they would do it. My Cognitive Release after Tigue was the same procedure but, as Judy put it, *like a spot clean.* "I mean, she's not scheduled for it or anything..."

The full treatment was like rebooting a hard drive. If she had this treatment, Celia would be the same person but also not at all.

We sat in silence, absorbing this, it felt like for a long time. "See if Trinie can get us in," I asked, "and soon? No one's going to tell us anything straight."

"It's all so sus," Azzie agreed.

We stepped out to the back porch. Azzie put her hand in her pocket and took out her miniature banana-shaped pillbox. She twisted it open and told me to hold out my hand. A red sphere rolled out. I took it, swallowed, and she took one too. A new edge eraser. A smoother smooth. As she got up to leave, I felt panicked. "You want to stay, stream some film clips or something?"

"Gotta go. Trinie's off and wants to spend some time with me." Azzie gave me a hug and started walking away.

I blurted out, "I miss you. I mean, I miss us three."
She lingered for a second. "I know, I know. I do too."

I felt like Celia's fall had taken out the three of us in some way. Nothing had been the same since that night. Celia's absence had magnified her essence, so much so that now we found we couldn't not talk about Celia, how she would offer up her antler, push it on us even, become cheeky if we refused. How much we missed it. How much I missed her. Azzie claimed she had a vial of Celia's tears that she kept in her bedside drawer (*when had she gathered them, I wondered, and why had I never heard about this before? what else between them did I not know about?*); I'd hung her portrait on my wall, the one with her eyes' thin slits, mounts of cheeks, hair around her head like a halo. She'd been in the hot tub the day I'd made it, had laughed at the idea of the currents from the gloves electrocuting us both, then we'd be sisters in death. I'd laughed too, it had sounded preposterous at the time, and yet...

Azzie and I held onto something else: a mutual sadness and anger, and we each wondered how much we were to blame for Celia's break. It made things tense. I hated it. Azzie admitted to me not long after that she wondered if I had tried hard enough to save Celia. As if I could have stopped it. I had thought about that moment over and over. We'd gotten too close, crossed a line, many lines that night. I'd never felt so alive, but also what was real about that night? A connection so elusive, formed by our chemical proximity and mutual sadness. Still, I ached. I was ravenous. This too had so much to do with this sadness.

COMMON QUESTIONS when taking *VALEDICTORIAN*

· · What form of _lyfe ENHANCE-ment is right for me?
 · WHAT PAIRINGS w/ VALEDICTORIAN root out excess, prevent caustic build-up?

· Can I stack VALEDICTORIAN with other supplements?
 · ··· ·how to prevent excess build-up and other blockages?

· ··· SEE HOW DELIXIR*V XR + delivers in real time
+++ HOW TO BEST ENHANCE your life+++

· · What do I do if I forget to take my DOSE?

· ··· ·Inconsistent dosing can lead to paradoxical effects, and other adverse effects including but not limited to mental instability, ambiguous thinking, and thought problems. Consult your prescriber for more information.

· · The following have been reported with use:
MIND-related problems
NEW OR WORSE BEHAVIOR
THOUGHT PROBLEMS****

· · VALEDICTORIAN is not for children under the age of 15. Do not take VALEDICTORIAN if you have a history of mental instability or deficits, it should not be mixed under any circumstance with certain supplements. CLICK HERE for the full list.

· Find additional supplements from LUMENA AFFILIATES

XIV.

We spent the following Saturday at the hospital. Trinie told her coworkers that Azzie and I were working on a school project and shadowing her for the day. Which means we had our pictures taken by security and wore sticker badges with our names and photos. Which means we wore scrubs and shoes with soft soles, kept pill cutters in our pockets, and hung stethoscopes around our necks. We adopted Trinie's pace, followed her two steps behind, consulted administration guides and took copious notes. She asked us to bring towels when a catheter fell out, and then to bring fresh bandages when a woman fresh from surgery began to bleed. I left to fetch more towels and when I came back the scent made my legs weak.

We went to pick up Liquid EnerG and bean paste cakes for the nurses at break. Lunch didn't come till midafternoon and when it did Trinie sat us down in the break room. "I'll take you to psych in just a minute. No funny stuff. Be calm and kind and try not to trigger any strong emotions, okay?" We agreed to withhold any signs of sadness for Celia's sake. We followed Trinie through long corridors that smelled metallic. When we arrived at the ward, we passed through three sets of doors and scanned the barcodes on our passes.

We found Celia in the crane room. There was nothing magical about this beige cube of a room with soft seats, its board games with soft-issue pieces, and its bookshelf lined with thin paperback volumes. Elegant birds with long legs surrounded by tropical plants were part of a mural on the wall. Celia sat on an ottoman with her legs crossed, hair up in a topknot. She sat deathly still, eyes closed, but looked up as we approached.

"HannahAzu! It's you! I could feel your vibrations approaching." We hugged, kissed cheeks, and told her she looked good despite the circumstances. Celia's face had narrowed and thinned. Her elastic waist athletic pants hung very loose and she kept scratching her wrists. She had a new intensity behind her eyes.

Trinie sat down next to Celia and gave her a hug. She asked which nurses and doctors she'd seen lately.

She threw her hands in the air, "Too many. Detestable, mostly. The nurses too. Weekend nurses are better, I don't mind them. Some are friendly, even."

Trinie didn't know any of the nurses she mentioned, they were mostly on-call. Celia said she felt F-I-N-E and wanted to leave. That she'd told this to her doctors and they disagreed, and that her parents sided with the doctors, mostly. Her father wouldn't acknowledge she was here. Her mother, when she visited, sat on the bed and asked her to pray while refusing to respond to any questions about coming home.

Trinie had a furrow in her brow. She said she'd leave us three alone, but she expected her Azulea and me to be back on her floor in twenty minutes.

We slipped back to Celia's room where she closed the door but had to keep it cracked. The concrete walls were sterile and drab. Her bed had baby blue blankets tossed across and an overhead lamp washed out any color.

We sat with Celia on her bed and didn't mention Samsun or Dr. Billy, or that we still hadn't heard anything more about Ms. Tigue. I told her about the horrors of my spa visit but also about Äsa and the massage.

"Hannah, what?!" Azzie exclaimed and elbowed me when I mentioned the AutoRox. I hadn't told her this part. I'm not sure why it hadn't come up.

"Sounds hot. I wish I could've gone." Celia was more of a spa person than I was. "But really," she continued, "let's cut the small talk. I love you two but I'm desperate. I am so sad but more so I don't want to be wiped clean—I mean, Erasure. Who am I without all my freak?"

"There's no plan still, it's all talk—right?"

Celia shook her head. "They seem serious."

"But why?"

"You tell me. They say my mind is labile, unstable. I don't want my hard drive fried. I've got to get out."

"Look, what happened that day, at the Center. Do you remember?"

Celia's face fell. "Some things. Anger overtaking me. They say I shorted. Mostly just red."

"As in the color?"

She nodded. "I am feeling much more myself."

"Yes, of course," I said.

"You know, there are eyes everywhere."

"Getting here was like entering a fortress," Azzie added.

I looked out the window to avoid Celia's gaze as I told her Azzie and I had been sending her good karma, but I didn't know what else we could do. I could see the factory smokestacks releasing their fat white breath.

Celia told us to hush and listen up. She'd made a friend who had helped make her aware of how she was monitored but couldn't say more. She was keeping tabs. Deliveries were made four times a day—with breakfast at 6, lunch at 11, and dinner at 4:30, another run came much later in the evening. The afternoon delivery was made on a cart that was switched out and the guy who exchanged the cart dashed in and out and was often careless. Nurses started giving the evening doses with dinner and during that time they left the station unoccupied. In the middle of the night, between two and five, everyone was sleeping, including the nurses on duty.

"This is good," I said. I said she didn't deserve this.

"All I can say is I have never had more time to think about things. I have never been so clearheaded."

This seemed true. Celia seemed keener, more strategic. She'd never been so certain about plans. She had an intensity in her face that wasn't just from losing the pudge from her cheeks. Her eyes were more animated.

"If anyone asks, you haven't heard a word of this. I'm telling you in case I need help. Would you?"

"Yes," I said.

Azzie agreed, as long as she could do it without involving Trinie.

Celia looked relieved, almost pleased, and said we should go. This was all she needed, and she didn't want to raise any suspicions. She would walk us back to the entrance. Celia told us that we had to move slowly and carefully—this was required on the floor, nothing that could rouse emotions was allowed.

"You can't be serious," Azzie hissed. I whispered that this kind of caution seemed ridiculous. Celia nodded. She'd had to observe it for weeks now. We surrounded Celia and plied her with goodbye hugs and kisses.

"Good luck," I whispered in her ear. "Here's to a

smooth flight out of here."

We didn't talk about visiting Celia when we returned to the general floor. We didn't talk about the visit later that afternoon or ever at all. I knew we both felt bad about the situation, the ways we wanted to intervene but couldn't. I felt guilty for leaving her on the ward. Like so much was my fault. I mean. All we could do was wait and see. We did continue to send good karma, but our meetings felt more somber. I had to try harder to make my energy lift toward her. I thought about Celia a lot even when I didn't say this.

XV. COUNSELING and INFORMATION

Judy did quite well for herself as the layperson's chemist. Client messages kept her device thrumming especially at the beginning and end of the school year. And now she had her four-step method: Seed Sprout Root Grow. It was that simple, like two plus two make four, that elegant equation. She was convinced that the universe, when reduced to its most basic elements, would be two plus two equals four. And yet some other mothers wanted to add two to nothing and come up with more.

She wanted to help, but help was often met with indifference. Look at Hannah, she thought. Her peril. The way Hannah's mind lit up like a brush fire when she'd started VALEDICTORIAN, then settled into a dazzling hum when she maintained a steady-state level. The V. coursing through her system would open doors even though—her dumb luck—it numbed her and she resisted. Judy wondered if Hannah had brought it on somehow, the way a negative worldview breeds negative outcomes, like a downward spiral. There must be an equation for that too. But, Hannah was defiant and an overreactor and refused to stay on course.

Test of wills. Nothing pained Judy more than Hannah's disregard for her work, her care, coming home to find her pills in the trash, watching her chipmunk tablets until she exited the room. It's like Hannah didn't know how easily her mind could go in the opposite direction. Entropy was a force of nature and called for maintenance and vigilance. This was why Judy was taking measures against it.

Judy had received a message from Crawford first thing that morning. Said they must confer about Hannah, skipping pills, switching up doses. Judy sent a swift reply—*message the details?* but thought—*no time for this.* She needed to cleanse her palate from the night before when Harold had sat staring out the window as she asked for his opinion on which dress would look better for filming?—she knew brown would match the color of SEED but also it was drab, too close to the color of her skin. She needed to look her best, zip, zip!

Harold's lack of response was worse than giving one she disagreed with. Had his absentmindedness grown? Sometimes it seemed like he was caught in his own skin. Was this what she'd married him for, was this the height of their intimacy?

She would take matters into her own hands. She was good at reality. Better than most. Which is why she turned her device to unreceptive, stripped down to her panties, then took her two-pill cleansing regimen, put on a cap and then sat in the chair netting, and wrapped it around her. The net provided electrical stimulation that accelerated internal processes. She needed to enforce her relaxation.

The alarm didn't go off! Her skin was baked. She couldn't wear that dress today anyway.

At least she felt focused.

She turned her device back on. Crawford had replied:

Best to meet

Briefly?

15 min max

Quarter to three?

Agreed

She opened her agenda, looked at her client lists. *Next stop: Bessa.*

Judy found Crawford waiting in the school canteen, its cascades of pills behind the shiny glass of vending machines. Two separate lines—one for snacks, the other for supplements—converged at the cashier. She grabbed a yolk + tryptophan tonic, made her way through, then looked around and asked if Hannah was coming too?

Crawford said no, he wanted to talk to her in confidence. He got up. He was sagging in places, his stomach, his neck. They walked back to the classroom and he stood over his desk, shuffled a few papers as she took a seat. She appreciated that he had special electron-emitting lamps. Good for focus.

He said he noticed Hannah had been downcast and disengaged of late. "Seems that a number of students are deviating from their regimens. How does she seem at home?"

Judy agreed. "I think she's still adjusting. With so many shocks, she's taking a while to even out. Have you spoken with Dr. Billy?"

"Not yet."

"She has an assessment with him coming up."

"That's good. Can I help?"

She didn't know. Her daughter was an outlier and thought rules didn't apply to her.

He tried again: "She seems. I don't know—lonely?"

"How could that be? She has more friends than me."

"I think she misses Celia, who, I mean, was a zombie before her breakdown—"

"And how does that relate?"

He just looked at her. "It worries me."

"Well yes, okay."

"Today in class we talked about corporate entities of the late twentieth century, and the shift of profits into the hands of the more able, and when I asked her to present her report on ExxonMobil, Hannah refused, asked—what does this have to do with me? Also brought up environmental catastrophe, then projected images of birds, some dead, slathered in oil."

Judy nodded. Hannah, of course she would project

images of dead birds, but what could she do? "It has been terribly difficult to offset the apathy she's developed. There were traces before, but now...."

Crawford nodded. He mentioned Hannah's interest in Romantic poets, Byron specifically for his interest in animals, living with a full zoo within his home. Llama, camel, goats, horses. Indoors. Not to mention the chimp family—

Those chimps. Why was Hannah so obsessed with them? She fretted that they'd been poached or some nonsense. The things her girl latched on to. Her obsession with Byron's exotic zoo of a household, borne of introducing her to Mary Wollstonecraft's *Vindication of the Rights of Women*, in an attempt to get her to take her schooling more seriously. She never could anticipate the way her ideas would backfire. She wanted to help Hannah find ways to wield power. As a woman, she would have to find practical applications for her intelligence and develop skills. She had to find scientific applications. She was too loosey-goosey, Judy thought.

Was Hannah following in Celia's path?

"Thank you for bringing this to my attention. How do we encourage her to find interests elsewhere?" she asked. "I mean, the animals, the poets, the deviation... Resistance to the common path can be... detrimental. I'm glad we had this talk."

"Yes, me too. It feels good to get this off my chest."

Crawford stood there like he'd told her some secret. He looked relieved and somehow expectant, like this was a transaction. Was she supposed to pat him on the back and say, good job?

It made her think back to his first semester teaching—she'd been the school liaison for new faculty about student regimens, covering Adverse Effects. Monitoring, Adherence. All of it. She'd met Crawford then; they were both much younger. They'd been in the mainframe server closet—doing what? She can't recall—they were surrounded by the machines, lights blinking, so much information processing, moving past them in megahertz (*she imagined it racing, like electricity, like lightning, but truly she had no idea*).

It was as if he could smell her needy self, her desire to hold more and more information, to shed her skin and let it run through her. She adjusted her skirt casually, or so she thought, and he said something like, *here let me help you*, and stood behind her as he stuck his fingers up inside her, her breath paused and he was kissing her neck, he was soon erect inside of her like a building, and she was like the world encompassing him. She wanted the world to fuck her, to collapse into a dream and she could ride it and harness its power. She wanted to fuck like that forever. But it ended. Swiftly. Without satisfaction. It always did. Now years later he had that same pained look and she didn't want anything to do with it.

133

She thanked Crawford for his time. She said she had to go. She had two more client visits and an evening appointment to shoot more video.

The lights were off when Judy got home that evening except for a distant glow, from which she could discern Harold was in his study and Hannah in the basement. Judy tried to think good thoughts before walking down the stairs.

She found Hannah sitting in the basement alone. Hair in her face, catatonic gaze. She was staring at a large gorilla—or was it a chimp?—hitting his chest with his hands and banging on a large aluminum barrel, then rolling it.

"What are you watching?" she asked.

"Oh that's the cousin, scaring off the other chimps. He's trying to make a move to challenge the dominant male."

She nodded but didn't understand, "...it's still just that one family?"

"Yeah, but I think he's at that age where he wants to kill his father and all of that. The male hierarchy is something they enact. They can be very aggressive, you know, bite off each other's hands and faces when they're pissed. This is nothing, really."

"I saw Crawford this afternoon. He wanted to talk. I think you know what it's about."

"Do I?"

Hannah just stared.

"I'm worried about you."

After a few minutes of silence Judy said, "Why are you deviating from your regimen? Are you trying to spite me?"

"No, I just don't like V."

"Can we talk about why you still need to take it? Do you want to discuss what you don't like?"

"Why can't we ever talk about what I do like?"

"These animals? That chimp—his future? What do you think it looks like? Do you want to join him in the wild?"

"Sure, I'd try."

"You don't know how it is out there or how to survive. Beyond the network of our society, our civility, things fall apart."

"I think these chimps are rather civil actually."

Can't get those ZZZZ's?

VIGILante for when you're short on sleep

XVI. ONTOLOGICAL IMPLICATIONS

In my Power, Politics, and Leadership class Mr. Crawford assigned a multimedia presentation on a leading historical figure. I proposed Percy Bysshe Shelley, the atheist who fled his homeland with the daughter of one of Judy's feminist heroes. Their lives were messy and awful and wondrous, forged through reading, writing, philosophizing, and passing their nights in deep conversation. But also, they were itinerant, errant, riding horseback through the pines, wandering always and trailed by so many ghosts of wives, lovers, and children left behind. Apparently, Shelley was better known as a poet when a poet was almost sacred, and he was a close friend of Byron's. Also: apparently, his heart didn't burn on the pyre. Apparently, his wife kept it with her until she died. Or something like that.

Crawford jotted back a quick approval: "Shelley's OK, stick to atheism, questionable otherwise, to bring in poetics and nature. Possible touch points include atheism/partnership with Byron/meaning of the infidel."

I hadn't seen Byron in this light. This boundary drawing made me want to explore what was off-limits even more. As I took notes, I found the more I wrote the more questions I had:

If passion is a byproduct of chemical reaction, how do enhancements alter our interpretation of cosmic occurrences?

What makes an experience? And is one type of experience more valid than another, i.e., natural vs. synthetic? Isn't it all chemical anyway?

Is a pill a form of experience?

If we alter the chemical, if the chemical alters our physicality, in taking do we alter the world?

Would Shelley have taken V.? Sparingly?

Does V. advance the poetic mind?

It made me wonder, what was a self? I mean really? It made me think of Descartes for some reason. We'd memorized his sound bite, "I think therefore I am," as justification for living mostly within mind/screen dynamics. But we never discussed what this meant. Or context. Without V., I sensed more of what was around me. It was the opposite of futurists, rocket ships, and supersonic speeds.

I'd never really thought about it previously, but what was the nature of Descartes's thinking? You know, before V., before the factory. How would Dr.

Billy's mind measure in comparison? Or what about the king and legislators and policymakers, the warmongers, the swindlers, the egoists so conscious of leaving their name in a textbook? I could feel their weight in my mind like an overstuffed attic.

MENISCUS: think at a faster cadence, clear excess bulk and tangles with speed

Later that afternoon we gathered for the weekly assembly, this time led by Dr. Billy. This was the first meeting I had attended since Celia was hospitalized. Judy said she was worried that this might trigger me.

I'd said I could handle it. Which was possibly a lie. But I wanted answers. For Celia, for Ms. Tigue, for me. They didn't call it a SIDE EFFECT. They didn't call it an ADVERSE REACTION. It was always Celia's "accident," Tigue's "mishap." Both were generally written off as labile, lonely, and unstable. No one asked openly if supplements had destabilized Celia, or if Ms. Tigue had started to encounter Cognitive Drift.

I entered through a side door and sat close to the stage but on the aisle. Azzie and Jeni came and Azzie sat beside me, her blue curls against the stark white seats, with Jeni on the other side of her.

Dr. Billy entered from the back of the room with Maxine trailing. She was obviously acting as his student assistant today.

He was wearing a tightly knit sweater covered in brown and orange geometric shapes; he was wearing gold laceless shoes. He entered without looking up and went straight to the front. He looked somber. Set books on his podium. Maxine disappeared through a side door and came back with two glasses of water.

He spent a good five minutes reviewing his notes. When he looked in my direction I pretended not to see.

I'd heard his lectures about V. so many times. He'd recycle the same stories that I could recite much of what he was likely to say without thinking: About our privilege as a fully augmented school. We were the first generation with fortifications in place, and because of this, we would make advances. In us he saw hope—for the future, the climate, in reversing the die-off of species, in uniting our isolated towns.

He stood up at the podium, and a silence fell over the room as he began to speak. His mouth opened and closed out of time with his words. Was it the PA or was my hearing not in synch? I heard "obstacles," I heard "tangled feet," I heard "A classmate's fall" and "concerning." I sat with Azzie, arm to arm, leg to leg. We had purposefully not taken any supplements before this, and would sit through it no matter how maddening, no matter what kind of pompous pontification of Dr. Billy's.

I was hoping to learn more about adverse reactions. About mental fragility and the overreactor. But these topics weren't mentioned. Billy mentioned chemical risk, that many people had asked him what he thought was behind Tigue's 'accident'—was it V.? Cognitive Drift? He didn't deny this but instead compared augmentation to air travel: "If the first planes that crashed had stopped us from flying, where would we be now?" Speed, velocity, and swiftness characterized our age. Minds had to keep up with digital modes of processing. It was a delicate balance, and in finding this balance a mind might fall, it could collapse and burn, but was this likely?

He shook his head no. He held his hands out to the room.

The room responded, "Nooo!"

"Consider the hand-drawn map," he continued, "the cartographers who used a compass and word-of-mouth and firsthand experience to create it. Think of the time it took to draw these maps and their vast inaccuracies. Now, think of the satellites equipped with cameras so powerful they can zoom in and watch a dolphin jump in the Pacific. What's the difference?"

I raised my hand.

"Yes, Hannah?"

"I don't know, but the dolphin is an endangered species."

"Your point being?"

"Perhaps we should care more about protecting them than admiring our ability to see them from great distances."

He said, "That's a curious idea," then went back to his blah blah blah about keeping perspective, safety measures, standards of use and more blah.

We'd all have cognitive check-ins next Tuesday, he announced. Upperclassmen, third and fourth years.

Yes, it was mandatory. Our supplementary records and journals must be up to date.

"Questions? Yes, Maxine?"

She asked a question about whether Mental Floss should be used weekly or biweekly? Did it make a difference?

I gave a side eye to Azzie. Maxine asked the most obvious questions.

Azzie raised her hand.

"Azulea?"

"So you're saying there's a connection between Tigue and Celia? That's what you meant when you talked about planes?"

He shook his head. "Not at all. Their cases are very different, really."

"But you're insinuating."

"I'm insinuating nothing my dear."

Jeni sighed audibly. I couldn't stand him talking to Azzie like this, either. Billy always dodged substance. So I interjected, "Okay but let's not sidestep the obvious? That Celia's now in psych? And Tigue, I mean, I don't even know. We're down two people, and you're talking about maps and planes crashing. Like are you saying V. caused this?"

"I know you're suspicious Hannah, but is there anything factual you're pointing to?"

This really infuriated me because of course he knew I wouldn't be able to point to anything specifically. He'd performed the Release.

"She was trying to tell us something."

"And what would that be, Hannah?"

His face was getting redder. Billy liked to exert a sense of cool control and hated to be challenged in the slightest way. I mean, in public especially.

"I just know what I've seen."

"Ok, let's not conjecture. We're following the scientific method. There is data." He said he'd give Maxine links to distribute and that we could read the studies once the assembly ended. But of course all of the studies would be issued by Lumena and the network of factories. It was impossible to know what they were omitting, if anything.

I tugged at Azzie's arm to get up and leave and she nodded like yes, as in leave, but also shook her head back to Jeni, whose arm was still in hers on the other side of her, like she couldn't untangle herself to leave in solidarity. And so I got up myself and left.

SIDE EFFECTS of VALEDICTORIAN include but are not limited to: Stuttered thinking, as in a needle skipping over a groove. Cluttered memories, nearing capacity. Fact abscesses without maintenance. Inertia, inability to think through. Nausea, dry mouth, tinnitus, feelings of discomfort, an inability to feel, feeling of wearing a second skin, a lack of desire, general. Other effects may include: nails bitten and chipped, facial picking, excessive exfoliation, excessive keyboard cleaning, an inability to inhabit oneself, restlessness.

XVII.

I had nowhere to be so I decided to walk home. I was steeped in frustration, with no answers from Billy. Azzie had stayed by Jeni's side when she should've come with me. I felt my device vibrate and hoped it was Azzie messaging. I'd wait to look.

My device buzzed again. I took it from my pocket. It was a reminder. In my bluster I'd forgotten I had a follow-up with Dr. Billy after the assembly, and I had to turn back.

The walls of Dr. Billy's office were the first indication he wasn't paying attention. They were striped lime, orange, and lemon, as if he wanted to wrap us in bland fruit colors. I am no fruit, I told myself because there was no one else around to listen. As I waited, messages popped up on my screen offering links to enhancement guides, offering health advice and asking questions like, *What fruit is your mind shaped like?*

The school nurse called me back. Her red glasses framed her face like a warning, her thin blonde hair was pulled back. Her smock-like lab coat was shorter than Billy's and had her initials *OXS* monogrammed in red. The O was for Olga. I followed her to a room. There were at least five of these rooms in a row. She instructed me to sit down and relax. She cuffed my arm and applied sensors to my forehead and chest.

"How have you been feeling lately, Hannah?"

"Fine."

"I see some notes here about a spa weekend with your mother, with a request to increase your mood stabilizer."

I sighed, "That's right."

"And so how is your mood?"

"Stable, I guess."

"I see from your journal entries of late you're keeping a proprioceptive practice and monitoring animal species. Conscientious. Do you participate in any mood-boosting activities?"

"I'd prefer not to."

She noted this. "You've listed fewer activities than at your last check-in. This is not an indication of improvement."

"I guess."

She raised her stylus and scribbled, then waited. She had the grayest eyes. Like chrome. Or maybe her red frames just made them seem so.

"I mean, I don't think it's relevant."

"Okay, that's curious." She noted this too. She set her tablet on the examination table, then handed me a device and stylus and told me that I'd need to answer a checklist as Dr. Billy's video walked me through the questions. She started the video and left the room.

On the screen Billy introduced himself and explained how he was a practitioner of the medical arts. I knew this. We were in an age of abundance, he explained. With our great abilities come greater responsibilities. He smiled, his cheeks shiny and plump, his silver curls tight. He wore a white lab coat. I wanted to ask a question but he kept talking. I stuttered. I stopped. This was not interactive. He went on.

Olga opened the door a crack and asked if I was doing okay. I said I needed help with the answers on my sheet. It's a yes-and-no checklist, she said. But I had too many in-betweens. She said not to hesitate with my answers, that overthinking was one of my largest problems.

I agreed, to some extent, but also knew if there were fewer problems I would have less to worry about. Fears came and whispered sweet nothings to me nightly, about how the earth would disintegrate without warning. My pills never stopped this panic, and I wasn't sure I wanted to pretend like nothing was happening. I worried about mutations from plastics, the rising temperature of the ocean, that melting icebergs would release a plague. I worried about the extinction of the honeybee and bananas and so many others. I wanted to think we would each die when we were ready. But I also knew it wouldn't happen that way. How was I now supposed to forget about this collapse, pretend like our imminent extinction wasn't a thing? There was no space to write this on the list.

Dr. Billy asked questions from the screen, which now showed my list:

Am I sleeping more than six hours a night?
  No.
Am I happy with my life?
  No.
Do I have friends?
  At this moment? It's hard to say.
Can I list my happiness on a scale of 1 to 10?
  Negative.

Am I receptive to practices that enhance my mood? What about chemical treatment?

The video ended. I sat there in the chair looking at the shelf in this closet of a room. There was a metallic figurine and a shelf of books that looked blah. A self-esteem workbook.

Dr. Billy entered the room and caught me looking at the book. He wore the same lab coat that he wore in the video but not the geometric sweater he had worn to the assembly earlier.

"So we meet again," he said in a way that didn't mask his underlying irritation.

I smirked. He lowered himself into the chair across from me, then looked over my answers.

"Just as I expected," he said, as he continued to look at his screen then looked up at me. "You didn't answer all of the questions."

I shrugged. "It seemed pretty obvious."

"I hear, Hannah, you still aren't feeling your best. Judy had mentioned concern for this too. Have you been engaging in mood boosting practices?"

"Olga already asked."

"Resistance is part of the common scourge."

"It's not that I'm 'against' it per se."

"Happiness is a choice. It's my choice. Could be yours too."

"Really, it's futile, and false, given our circumstances."

He widened his eyes as if out of the habit of trying to make the right faces to perform his empathy. "Ah, I see," he acknowledged.

He told me he was concerned about my mental stability. That he worried my dose of VALEDICTORIAN might be too much for me. But before pulling back he wanted me to try something else. It would preserve my pineapple mind. *I am no jam*, I thought.

Dr. Billy told me I have three of the six indications on this checklist for Azpire. That I am in ill spirits, feeling blah? I said, I guess. He asked me to divulge what type of blah, whether it's an everyday blah like a meatball falling on the floor and accidentally stepping on it, or a blah blah blah of hot air that sits in my stomach that makes me feel bloated.

I declined. I had told him plenty on the sheet.

"A paucity of words is a fourth indication."

He told me I needed a stabilizer. Especially with my history of Cognitive Release. That there were signs that my mind was regressing. I was in a delicate place. He told me to imagine building a fortress and the scaffolding needed for support. That's what the stabilizers would do. He didn't want me to crash. He smiled while saying this. He told me he was transmitting a script. That Olga would send more information. I could pick it up at the dispensary in 20 minutes.

"Take two twice a day, in the morning and before bed. You can add an extra midday if you're especially stressed." He said to take it on an empty stomach, with a full glass of electrolyte enhanced water. He recommended I begin with 5mg doses and increase until I no longer experience anhedonia.

I asked what he meant.

"Utter joy, you will feel it again dear."

Qualities of memory on V:

Flat thinking.
Acquisition.
Pattern recognition.
Retrievable, often quickly.
And yet.

Harold's gaps were growing, soon enough they would spread to encompass his world. He had spaces when he couldn't find the right word to fit. Not complicated words like *thermodynamic*... not when he was speeding through at a steady clip but every so often   words flew off   like a bird:

Instead of saucer he thought   *circle in front of me ... flat surface for ... cup ...... holds tea*. Instead of ignition ... *place to.... insert key*. He waded through so many words to describe just one thing. He became flustered... the more flustered ... the more aware ... of all the words. None right. Many flocked to replace the disappeared.

Little ruptures led   to cracks   fragmentations to breaks. Inevitable system failure. He knew too well that systems collapsed. At his age how many words did he have? ... a college-dictionary? ... at least perhaps ... an engineering index?

Words, they slipped like they had no care. Like Harold had offended. He'd taken for granted the ways they'd always been there. Words for objects, chair was always chair. But now without that middleman   he was swimming ... gasping. He'd published papers over his career. Was once a forerunner   and now ...

... so difficult to talk to Hannah. Horrible things were happening. Sara Tigue and now her friend. He wanted to say   hold on to relevant memories! It was difficult now he was so clumsy. Some days his mind crawled at snail's pace. Some he could run through ideas, sprint even, though never as fast as he used to. VALEDICTORIAN after forty-five? Didn't work. Hit a wall. Some studies showed augmentation made memory tangle.

Read a brief that morning at desk while working ... a mission to Mars and a rocket made it some of the way   something happened ... exploded? ... intercepted? ... an astronaut died? He wasn't sure but it was dire.

Words failed and he felt something   general shapeless like color or sound   a drum in the distance. Hannah greeted him that evening when he came home.

She asked, "How was your day?"

Mind searched ... saw an explosion. He stood atop a landfill of language. Impossible to find words but soon enough "Troubled mission."

She nodded. Smiled. He appreciated that she tried ... he saw she had a sweet heart   wished for more words like *Excuse me during this seven-second delay* ... freeze tag ... a game. Wanted to ask about her day.

Hannah had walked away.

In the observatory no words just   sky   star   moon
like black-and-white cookie. One side dark... Tried to
photograph and looked like a fuzzy half circle.

Found   Hannah   downstairs.   Always   before
screens ...... and her blue-haired friend wasn't here
lately.   He   wanted   more   words   to   ask
areyoulonely? So much time Hannah spent face
scrunched and scowling.

Showed the photo of the moon and Hannah smiled.

If only he'd not fall further.

Empathy was an easy word. Empathy was a name
that was straightforward, it wasn't tricky or showy or
seductive. Harold had written EMPATHY in notepad. Saw it again after dinner. A reminder. Excused
himself and sat in study ... through the window gazed
at smoke always rising.

He programmed the car to take him to a store. Out
of the way but not too far. Didn't want to run into to
see   so much ... ladies ... oh everything. To have to
remember and not. Not was the worst, like a stomach
punch.

He walked to the counter and pointed to the notepad.

"Do you think?" he asked "... yes?"

"We have Empathy in stock, an ample amount of
40mg caps. It's a popular one."

"Mmm-hm."

"Like some?"

Harold nodded and checked off **30-DAY SUPPLY**. Then sat in a chair out of the way. The counter had a line. Men and women with blank faces poking at pads. Was there ever not a busy night? Behind the counter the man in white jacket held knife and slid rolly circles across. *Roll roll roll* like wheels ... greasing ... machine. The motions the man made and so many assistants working in sync like ... like a music video.

Count count count he was keeping time ... he was metronome.

Harold nodded ... yes the rhythm it did something. *Click click click.*

What was a body at rest? Not dead but with synapses firing in equal but opposite directions?

XIX. QUALITY ASSURANCE

In the morning the factory workers lined up outside for the start of the first shift, which began in fifteen-minute intervals. Workers stared at their reflections in the tall glass doors. When the doors opened the workers walked in, down a hall, and gathered in a large room lined with lockers and benches. The sound system emitted a positive buzz from above.

All entries were monitored. Signs were posted:

GOOD PRACTICES MUST BE MAINTAINED
AIM FOR POSITIVE PRODUCTIVITY
WITH TEAMWORK WE ACCOMPLISH THE IMPOSSIBLE

All clothes were removed, folded, and held in a locker until shift's end.

White suits were put on in their place and worn in sterile areas.

Each morning a new suit was donned. Legs first, then arms, then zip, then tie.

Cover hair, tuck beard, cover mouth, cover feet.

Wash hands under running water: soap, rinse, then dry.

One door closed before the next unlocked. One door led to another and another, down a corridor. Bodies moved through, entirely covered except for eyes and necks.

Hands turned switches, recorded temperatures. Moved containers filled with powders, scooped and weighed. Blue screens turned purple as the queue of products grew, and soon began to blink red. *Work faster! Work faster!* they said. Speed first, but also accuracy.

No error is acceptable. No error is an anomaly. The factory practices are good practices. Only the finest workers, only the purest product.

Distributed to neighboring towns and villages. Inquire at your local counter, order through your online retailer.

Good practices are sober, clean, and sterile. Good practices are controlled, replicable and assayed often. Good practices assure the chemical composition is not adulterated.

From the delivery dock came box after box. One followed another on the conveyor belt, an underground birth canal.

And so on. And on and on they went. And yet.

Ingredients came from all over: sea extractions, valley dirt, freight from foreign ships. All contents delivered were first stored in a warehouse that spanned a full acre.

The conveyor belts delivered each box to a specific destination. From there the contents were taken, unpacked, and altered.

The workers made so much with their beakers of liquid chemical, dry ice, pulverized powders.

When the break time bell rang a trickle of bodies exited labs through the series of lochs, in the opposite way they entered. White-clad bodies gathered in a hall with tables the size of tennis courts. Most of the chairs remained empty. There was never enough time to exit, rest, and return to the station.

Workers were only allowed to leave once the next shift arrived. There were no exceptions.

These were sacrifices that had to be made. For the good of the people, for the good of the company.

Health and well-being first, they said.

Answers to all sources of inquiry were readily available, in chemical form. Manufactured and distributed widely.

There were pills for sinners and scandal-makers, pills for do-gooders and the uptight, pills against neuroses, inhibitions. There were pills for perfectionists and Type A's, for habitual B-listers and bruised egos. Pills for learning to love yourself, to accept that there's no meaning beyond the everyday. Pills to cure loneliness, to learn to be alone, pills to stop yelling at sports games, pills to soothe, to make you want to do. Pills to finesse, to forget about otherness, to fill absence, emptiness. Pills for everyone under the sun.

We are one pharmaceutical, under God, with the permission of our insurance provider (see your policy for details or call 1-800*RX*SOLUTIONS). Prior approval may be necessary.

In the factory, the computers were down. The assembly line was stopped every three hours for quality assessment, but the conveyor belt hadn't budged since noon. Glitch in the system, someone said. It could last an hour or two or stretch for a day. Maybe longer. Back-up systems were in place but would likely take just as long.

On a good day the pills rolled in a steady march like an army, each with its own target. Together they advanced.

Today wasn't a good day. A rumor spread among the workers faster than viral: a rogue chemical tainted the mix, an adulteration yielded the entire batch unfit. The morning's vat of components remained untouched, now covered with plastic. The vat would have to be emptied and stripped, the batch would be decontaminated and restarted from scratch.

We regret to say that this may cause some unforeseen delays.

From the other room Harold heard his wife woman-scream, "adulteration at the factory!" Adulteration is not a form of adultery. He had no hand in it and yet it seemed that she was blaming him for even this. These two things, whichever, both, neither, held no interest for him. If it were up to him, their lives would've been like two newly formed stars forever held in a potential state: before the energy burned away, before they combusted against the night sky.

None of that spark remained. No mark except meteorite, that drastic fall, that death wish.

However much he liked the ladies who smiled at him with toothy grins, Harold generally didn't notice them. It wasn't in him. His wife, she'd horned him again and again; he the ox, sadness filling his balloon heart when he gave it thought. This pill made him so full with feeling. Made him feel closer to the door, his wife an empty closet.

Judy, his Jude, would have traded him for others he was sure, if only she didn't despise so much mess-making. She was a keep-it-together kind of lady. You could be sure she would clean it away.

If they were an atom, he thought, yes an atom, then she was the proton, he the neutron, and Hannah, their electron spinning…

Judy came in and sat next to him distraught. He tried to convey his calm to her as they sat, all will resume as normal soon. *The best manufacturing practices*, he reminded her. Hannah hadn't come home yet. This ate at her. She hadn't touched her plate of heart and liver at dinner, her salad wilted in front of her. She shook her device, no messages. She texted rapidly. They waited. She didn't laugh at his wives tale about watched kettles.

The later it became, the more rapidly she fired. He tried to bridge the distance by rubbing her shoulders, offering to get in the car and search for the girl.

"No use. I can't even ping her," Judy said. Apparently the girl knew how to lose them when she wanted. Judy sat straight line and deflected. Plans were like a grid. They must be rigid. But they were also like a sieve.

As long as Harold took the pill he could sit and listen. Not always with words, not even half the time. He felt his failure but not only words fill distances.

Time passes and creates more gaps.

He left Judy on the couch and got in the car. Set his device to search mode, circled blocks while trying to sync with Hannah's device. Smart girl didn't want to be found. He didn't really care if she were an apricot pineapple melon pie. As he looked out the window he saw sidewalks, empty houses, and the ominous glow from Factory Hill.

The adulteration had spread. Adulterated powders were to be discarded in containers marked HAZARD-OUS WASTE. All other powders were placed in the vault that was then sealed airtight.

Evacuation orders were in place. Workers were to follow procedures for cleaning and removal. Workers were given times to depart. Orderly exit, every fifteen minutes. Two pills and one plastic bag were handed to each as they vacated their places. A quick and efficient exit was imperative. They were to remove their suits, place them in the bag, place it in HAZARDOUS WASTE then walk to the closest emergency post.

White tents already formed a circle around the factory. The workers saw this as they exited, their white uniforms flooding the land like milk spilling over the hill. They gathered at the stations, floodlights beaming down. No one could say what had happened, just had blank faces, blank stares, arms in the air. They sprayed their outerwear with powder, then lined up for showers.

Precautionary measures. No reason to worry! Just in case! It's not a problem, just a run-of-the mill... said the supervisors, the healthcare officials, the facility managers. They were to be taken at their word.

The burning had started in the outer stations after the last employees had fled. The fires consumed stores of suits and booties and beard covers and somehow grew up and beyond to fill the stations and circle the factory. Helicopters hovered over the fire and the workers gawked at the footage on their devices, as the flames dancing behind them grew (*face away*, they were told). It looked like there was a larger burner under the hill, as this burning spread with intent, through trees and leaves and blowing with the winds. Were large fans hidden within? How was this happening?

How this was happening: The fire surrounding was soon mirrored within, with flames bursting from windows. Rubber melting, causing shriek and shelter, glass windows popping, machines lowing and hissing as they sweltered. Fire filled all empty spaces, spread into the depths of the maze, except, who knows how long it took for the lochs to give. Fire the destroyer, the eviscerated structure falling in, falling into itself.

The factory was transformed into a torch in the night sky, and still smoldered with the morning light.

NOTICE: BACKORDER
TAKES EFFECT: IMMEDIATELY
LASTS: INDEFINITELY

A CATASTROPHIC EVENT HAS BEFALLEN THE LUMENA CORP AND THE SURROUNDING COMMUNITY.

LUMENA'S MANUFACTURING ARM WAS DESTROYED IN A FIRE LAST NIGHT. THE INTEGRITY OF THE BUILDING HAS BEEN COMPROMISED AND ALL MANUFACTURING PROCESSES HAVE BEEN SUSPENDED.

MEASURES WILL BE TAKEN TO RESUME PROCESSES AS SOON AS POSSIBLE. WE HAVE ALREADY CONTACTED OTHER FACILITIES FOR TEMPORARY RELOCATION.

ALL ENHANCEMENTS, AUGMENTATIONS, AND SUPPLEMENTS MANUFACTURED BY THE LUMENA CORP FACTORY ARE IN SHORT SUPPLY. ALLOTMENTS WILL BE MADE AVAILABLE AS POSSIBLE.

WE APOLOGIZE IN ADVANCE.

WE CANNOT FULFILL NEW OR OUTSTANDING ORDERS UNTIL FURTHER NOTICE.

WE URGE THE COMMUNITY OF LUMENA HILLS TO RELEASE STOCKPILES SO THAT THOSE IN NEED HAVE ACCESS TO SUPPLIES.

BACKORDER: VALEDICTORIAN   DURATION: INDEFINITE

BACKORDER: MENTAL FLOSS   DURATION: INDEFINITE

BACKORDER: EMPTEZ   DURATION: INDEFINITE

BACKORDER: DELIXIR   DURATION: INDEFINITE

XX. CHEMICAL INSTABILITY

A dark plume engulfed the factory. It's just what I'd imagine my brain would look like if it were dashed open. If my mind continued in this direction, I'd become what—a pumpkin and a dimwit? An apple, solid, sweet, and wholesome? Or worse, a fruit rotting. I couldn't imagine performing the same laborious tasks day after day, organizing information, pouring pills into containers and placing containers into machines, or a future in administering customer satisfaction surveys, spent asking, *Do you have a moment to tell me about your experience at the dispensary today?*—What kind of future would that be anyway?

Though I wondered what kind of future any of us had here in Lumena. Here on this hill, a speck on this planet, mid-Sixth and careening toward finish. Here, at the beginning of my own life, was the beginning of the end of life as any of us have known it. The sky was gray and all seemed bleak.

I made my way past the charging stations and dispensary windows, their neon orange capsules always lit. Outside, so many suits spread across the plaza: all were tap tap tapping at their keys, whispering into where, what receiver, the ether?—all just talk talk talking, their words light as a whisper in the wind, whispering as if trying to allure me. I heard wisps of *hello love, howdy, hey loser, order now, burning down, devastating, staggering, connected, dropping? breaking up, bit rate ISP, rate your trip, greater frequency, greater speed.* I swear I could hear synapses humming with intake, processing messages, melodies, IMs, DMs, swipes, all firing so rapidly. All of this unfolding happening—in the air, in the pinpoint, in the spaces between, or perhaps even within us.

We're always moving as fast as the world is rotating. But what was left to hold on to? "Not much, not much," Dr. Billy had said about what I could do. Beyond more capsules, pills, and tablets. I was well on my way to downgrading—not much could be done besides taking and waiting. Billy's first direction was to keep my mind at rest. *A body at rest is less likely to fall.* To take AZPIRE. And if that didn't work? *Sedate.* At least that was one of the treatments detailed in the packet Olga had sent me. It required being placed in a semi-hypnotic state for a stretch of days, weeks even—to alleviate the mental weight. *I would prefer not to,* I'd said, to Billy, to not do any of this. And he'd smiled his menacing smile. Of course he did. That's when I'd started to run.

The smoke clouds over the hill were darker than I'd ever seen as I ran to the bank of the river. And as I ran I could hear Judy's voice in my head. My device shook, as if on cue. I took it from my bag. I could see

Judy mouthing words. I could make out "factory." I could make out "falling." I shoved the device back into my bag, but somehow this unmuted her and I could hear her voice, muffled: "I implore you—come home! Honey, please, you must take ALL OF YOUR MEDS. Do you hear me? ALL of them. ... I mean, what if.... I mean, once you're rotting there'll be no stopping!"

These last words echoed in my head. I saw myself a putrid fruit, bottom rotting and flies abuzz in the noonday sun.

As I approached the river's edge, I saw its banks dotted with tufts of white. More tufts were floating downstream, almost like dumplings. I ran onto the bridge and stopped midspan by a brown case atop the guardrail, with the words BREAK in EMERGENCY written across glass. Behind the small pane a life preserver glowed orange like the pill in the dispensary window.

Whoever had placed a life preserver at this precise location knew the effect of great heights on the desire to leap. Dread overcame me. Was this not an emergency? Suddenly it seemed like I'd been led here to this exact location. I broke the glass and took the preserver. It hadn't occurred to me that I'd do this just now but this was just one surface of so many things that needed breaking.

I wished someone would've also placed a vial of

Delixir behind the glass so I could down a handful, and then leap and soar and take in the skyline in a brief wondrous flash before falling so fast. I rummaged through my pockets. All I had was AnxietEZ. I swallowed one, then a few, and climbed up onto the rail. I looked out at the billows of smoke before me. I waited a minute, then closed my eyes and dropped the preserver into the river. I stood on the top rail and dangled a foot over. I stood there, eyes closed, trying to will myself over into the dumplings below. But I couldn't. My arms shook as I clung to the case, as I somehow guided my feet back to the concrete. I was ashamed by my inability to take a great leap in any one direction.

I could see bodies swarming on the hill, and white tents forming a line at the top. I wanted to run to witness the chaos but my chest felt so heavy. I sat on the concrete and then I took my device out and watched Judy's face over and over, her jaw opening and closing and opening again. Suddenly her teeth grew dark, and two chimps emerged from behind my mother's molar. They wrestled onto her tongue. With her next scream, they covered their ears.

I closed my eyes—was this really happening?

I spied another chimp in the shadow of her cheek. This one had a large stick and started banging on a filling; it made a tinny sound that became maddening. Made my head throb.

This couldn't be happening and yet....

I watched this all play on while Judy's mouth yammered on and filled with capsules of cream & navy, peach & purple, sea green & blue, these capsules filled her hole of a mouth until they started spilling out and breaking, releasing liquid magentas and purple streams, dark ash falling. Judy had a halo of smoke and glow, she looked like the patron saint of something sordid.

The air smelled of burnt vinegar. I heard Celia's voice in my mind repeating, *what good are wings if you don't fly?* I saw her in a green gown, climbing through the hospital window, tiptoeing on its ledge, then falling.

I saw Tigue's face before she turned her gaze toward the hill. I saw her platinum wig, her pearly teeth, a pomegranate seed rolling.

Tigue whispered as I held her hand. She said she saw a light beyond the factory.

And then: the warmth of a body beside me. A pair of legs, an arm on my back. Curls against my cheek. A sharp, familiar scent, maybe patchouli? I turned my head and saw Azzie's eyes focused, her mouth covered, her concern.

She said she'd come to look for me when I wouldn't answer her messages. She said she'd been sitting beside me on the side of the road for more than fifteen minutes. That I wasn't moving and staring straight ahead. That she'd put the mask over my mouth and I hadn't responded.

I told her she was crazy, and she said she wished that explained it. I felt her hand on my back. I was surprised how this calmed me.

"Toxic crosswinds," she said. "Factory has burned."

"Burned?"

"Incinerated. Collapsed inward."

"Wait. What?" I gasped. How could it?

"Chemical substances released. Indoors mandatory. They say we have nothing to worry about. Will blow over."

"Will it?"

"We need to get going. Many are sick. Shallow breath, heaves and sweat. You should get checked."

"I'll be okay."

"Just come with me, and we'll go see Trinie. She'll make it quick."

I agreed, but we couldn't get a car—so we started walking. I could move on my own but my mind went woozy with small decisions, like which way to proceed at each corner. All the stop lights looked to me like they were blinking.

"Were any of the workers hurt?" I asked.

Azzie didn't know. She asked if I'd been in touch with Judy. Judy had messaged her.

I didn't want to think of Judy. I mean, the chimps, her scream. What was that anyway? I felt like I'd been hit with a sack of bricks.

Azzie screamed. She was staring at her device's screen.

"Azzie. Please. I can't deal."

"—listen!" She shoved her device at me. I held it to my ear and heard Celia's voice clearly. She said she'd left the hospital, and that she was on her way—to where? She didn't say.

I gave it back and mouthed—"Celia?! How?"

Azzie dialed the number she'd called from. She got an old man on the line who said, yes, he'd lent his phone to a girl—where was she, you ask?—well she'd disappeared. Did we know how crowded it was, with all these people trying to breathe the same air?"

"How, now?" Azzie repeated to no one in particular.

Was it just a coincidence that I'd envisioned Celia's escape—the seeming connection of these two improbable events? I was in no place to assess.

The hospital lot was full of bodies waiting, cars lined

up to get in. If I were doing their portraits, I'd have attempted to capture the fear on these faces covered with scarves, mouths obscured. Two attendants flanked the entrance, handing out masks.

As Azzie led me through the hospital corridors, I could hear the patients' labored breathing from behind partitions, the long wheeze and the *swoshwoshwosh* of the breathing machines beside the beds lining the halls. She led me upstairs to the medical unit where her mother was stationed. Trinie told us to wait in the break room and gave us a code to unlock the door. Azzie let us in, got me a cup of water.

It's passing, she had said. Though who could say? The factory hadn't burned before. How long would we inhale this darkness? How many days would we have to wear masks before forgetting what it was like to walk outdoors without them? How many terns and finches were falling, failing to catch their breath?

I sat on a puke brown padded bench—why did everything in the hospital elicit sickness? The view up here was much like below. More smoke, the top of the hill glowing like a hot coal. Truth was, part of me was glad the factory was burning.

"You okay if I leave you?" Azzie said. "Try to find Celia, you know?"

I nodded yes, implored her to, and swung my arm to shoo her. She ran to the door, then turned and blew me a kiss. I sat for a while waiting, looking at the coats flung over chairs, the trash can with wipes and gloves in a heap overflowing, the half-eaten plates of food strewn across the table.

Trinie flew into the room, harried, with her hair back in a loose braid and wearing space cadet scrubs. She had a rolling cart that held a monitor and a tray. She took a clear plastic contraption from the top, held it to my mouth and told me to inhale deeply then exhale into the opening. She groped me and poked me, and placed my fingers in plastic clamps, then held a stethoscope to my chest. She worked quite quickly.

"You don't have the heaves, kiddo," she said when she was done. She paused and asked me what had happened with Billy.

I stumbled in responding, but was able to spit out, "Mostly talk. Fear of downgrading, or something like that."

"I don't like the sound of it."

She was the only adult I knew who at times seemed skeptical of Dr. Billy's supplement schedules and treatments. Something to do with increasing numbers and patients not recovering, conversations she'd had with other nurses. Azzie had told me Trinie thought he was maybe too enticed with his experimental treatments.

Trinie shook her head and muttered. *Sham*, she said. Or was it *Shame*? Difficult to say.

"Should I be worried?" I asked. "About today?"

"You need to rest. When was the last time you took your V.?"

"This afternoon."

"Before that?"

"Not for days." Not unusual, for me at least.

"Then don't again. Not for a while. Let your mind rest. Try to not take in too much, feel too much, over-work your synapses."

"And how? I mean, especially now..."

"Take a relaxant. I'll give you a few. Azzie needs to stay with you. Lock yourself in a closet. Don't look at the news."

I laughed, "What about Judy?"

She looked up at the clock, and started cleaning the tray. "Perhaps," she said, "you should avoid her too."

Facts tough as diamonds collide, obliterate images that vanish, one into another. Mind receives files, information, waking hours. Absorb and sort ideas, memories. On-screen: herd of elephants—scroll—tear gas and riot shields—scroll—quarantine—scroll—fires raging over forest and land—scroll—disappear.

XXI.

I texted Azzie on my way out. *Released me. Free from heaves for now—Where are you?*

I saw the crowd again, their faces covered. They looked to me like they were hiding, this mob waiting outside in air unfit to breathe.

Azzie replied: *Found Celia. Not how you'd think. Back at home, wouldn't get in a car with me so we walked here s-l-o-w-l-y ~/_:++ /~*

I had new messages from Judy, too. She had to perform an emergency inventory for the Learning Committee. Would be late. She asked if I would get in touch? *Your father is very worried*, she said.

I relayed this all to Azzie.

Message Harold if you want to. What's the worst it will do?

I just couldn't bring myself to.

When I arrived at Azzie's, she led me through the house to the couch where Celia was spread out. She was still wearing her hospital gown and had a blanket over her legs. She looked to me like she was sinking into herself. The dark circles around her eyes made her look even more doelike. We examined each other for a moment. I told Celia I was sorry for all she'd endured, but at least she'd gotten out?

"Don't give me some bullshit, Hannah."

I stepped back, looked to Azzie who just gave me a dumb look.

"Um, it's good to see you too," I said.

"Sure, sure. Look, you don't know the torture I endured. And now I hear you think you have problems? *Ha.* I hear you're crushing on Azzie. She's impermeable, didn't you know?"

WTF. She sounded like some jealous lover. I felt like I'd walked into a glass door.

"I don't know what you're talking about." I turned to Azzie, who stood in the doorway, for some cue.

"I'm sooo tired," Celia said suddenly. "I need some shut-eye. Just a little—don't take offense, dears." She lay back down.

I turned around and whisper-hissed, "What's that all about?"

Azzie motioned me to the next room and whispered, "I don't know. She's worse off than I thought."

"Where'd you find her?"

"Just beyond the parking lot. She was walking through the brush. Dressed only in that gown, in her bare feet."

"Was she like *that* to you—?"

Azzie shook her head no, said they'd talked on their way back. "She just seemed very concerned about being seen and said she has some place to go. Made me promise that I won't interfere. And not tell you. She kept muttering under her breath. *Gotta fly the coop, mourning dove, coo.*"

"You're shitting me."

Azzie shrugged. "You know how she can play stupid, but worse."

"She's batshit?" I wondered if she'd had Erasure.

"Yes, no? Batshit but on point. She wouldn't let me order a car."

"There weren't any."

"I was able to flag one down. She wouldn't get in. Said she didn't want to be tracked."

"So you walked?"

"Yes."

"And?"

"And what?"

"What did you say about me?"

"About us?"

"Yes."

"Nothing, really. Just things have been weird."

"And?" I was good at asking questions. Less so at articulating the shape of my mind.

"I don't know what that was about. I love you both. You know the three of us don't keep secrets."

"Except you said you wouldn't tell me."

"But I did tell you, silly."

We'd once said we'd never keep secrets from each other. I was beginning to wonder. It felt like there was something more. "She's mad."

"Possibly?"

"I mean, mad at me."

"We're all on edge."

"Okay, but I'm still pissed at you."

She gave me a look. I felt so many things.

"Hey, okay—but tell me, what happened with Trinie?"

"*Relax*, is what she said. That I don't have 'the heaves.' She gave me a relaxant and told me to rest."

"Yeah, she messaged me. Told me to look after you."

"You don't have to be *my* savior too."

I heard Celia stirring in the other room. We went back in and she was perched on the sofa's edge. Her gaze was empty. Her hair was matted on the back of her head.

I looked to Azzie for a cue. She looked perplexed.

She looked past me as if she didn't register my presence. Her right foot was shaking. She kept scratching her face.

Azzie stepped in, placed pillows behind her back, and laid her back down on them.

Celia immediately pulled herself up again. "I must be going."

"No, no. Just relax. You can't go out in this."

"Game's changed."

Azzie sent me out—or tried to. Really, I left the room gladly.

Don't take it personally, Azzie had said as I left, but how could I not? This was not at all like I'd imagined Celia's return. Our conversation should've been filled with talk of sexy psych residents, perhaps she'd made out with one or two by now? Complaints of the bland hospital food, gossip about other inpatients. I'd thought that set free, Celia would be clear-headed and strong, like when we visited. Not like this.

I thought of Celia with her antler, always slightly overeager to fawn over some dude too full of himself—dark eyes, lithe frame, her descriptions had been the best, her disclosure of secrets: the shape of an ass, thickness of their prowess, the ways it would hang, hidden tattoos, acne on the back, testicles like hacky sacks. I had an entire catalog of loins in my mind and I'd never seen a dick in my life. Not that I cared to. The way Celia talked of dicks they sounded more like snakes. The old Celia would've loved to hear that a thought-to-be-extinct-two-headed-snake had just been discovered alive in the Amazon. I desperately wanted to tell her this or indulge in some other nothingness.

When I came back, Celia smiled and now seemed to welcome me. "Let's try again? Excuse my goose."

"You know I do." I walked over and gave her a hug. Her body felt like a sack of bones.

She shook her head as she held her hand across her

arm and a deep purple bruise she paid no attention to. I figured it was from her IV's.

I asked how things had been since our visit.

She said she mostly felt numb. She couldn't tell what caused it but her neural network had been thinned, or so she'd been told.

"—did it hurt?"

She shook her head. She looked directly at me. We held a flicker of connection before her face fell back into vacancy.

I wondered when they'd cleared her head and what they'd filled it with. I told her I wanted to do her portrait. She consented. I got my pack, took out my gloves and stretched them over my fingers. Celia pulled her fuzz of hair back in a knot. She said she didn't know what she'd been given on the ward. They'd just brought her pills and liquids she had to swallow. If she refused, she'd get an injection and her mind would be in a haze for days.

She seemed like she was talking from a faraway place.

I placed my hands on her cheeks, ran them over her eyes, her soft lips. As I felt the contours of her face I thought of all of the other times we'd done this. Judy's words, *death mask*, kept echoing in my mind.

I asked if she remembered what happened with Samsun and that day at the mall. The SUV. She nodded and laughed. "Like a shard of glass. Like watching a movie starring someone else."

Azzie entered the room carrying two blankets and a plush owl. She placed the owl under Celia's feet, "Is it too hot?" She explained that the owl held a hot water bottle.

Celia said, "It's fine. Hot is good. I can feel it."

Azzie placed one blanket over Celia, and the other by her feet, then took a seat by her head on the armrest. "I'll take good care of you."

I suddenly felt adrift. Wasn't I her ward now? I watched as Azzie placed her hand on Celia's neck and caressed her hair.

She wasn't her mare. I gritted my teeth.

"I don't want. I don't need," Celia said. She said she had a friend to meet.

"Like where would you even go?" I asked.

She made us promise not to repeat anything about what she was about to say. She said a weekend nurse had taken interest in her, listened to her pleas to avoid Erasure, and had taken her aside one night. Said she could help. But only if Celia wanted. And if she did, she'd have to be brave.

"Of course I wanted to," she said

"But how—?"

"She gave me tips, let's say. Helped me on my way."

"What now?" I recalled she'd said something alluding to this when we'd visited, but I hadn't thought anything of it.

"I can't say. I don't know more than I'm going to meet her. Someone. Beyond Lumena, I think."

"You're kidding, right?" Azzie looked almost frightened.

Celia remained straight-faced. She said the nurse had given her coordinates for where to meet.

I entered them into my device. They were far—in the foothills just before the mountains. The hike could be done in a day, if done quickly, the nurse had said.

None of us had traveled that far. None of us had gone past the factory, really. We had all been there on field trips and watched the black conveyor belts, the vats filled with powders. We'd watched how they were measured, tamped into capsules, mixed into pastes, and cut into pills, cascades of them. There were excursions, too. The spa. Loggers went to cut down trees and the naturalists, to replant them. Scientists, researchers, factory employees. No one else bothered.

"There's nothing in the forest but trees," I said. This is what Judy had always told me.

"I'll be fine."

"This all sounds très sus to me," I said.

Celia shrugged. "Getting out is enough. It was the only thing that made sense in there. She thinks the factory and Billy are misguided, says real change comes from elsewhere."

"Elsewhere—what does that even mean?" Azzie crossed her arms like she did when she was staking her ground. She knew as well as I where elsewhere was.

"Look," I said. "Does she know you're coming?"

"I have to message her."

"Now?"

"Soon. Not too soon. All must be in place before I do."

"And you'll get there how?"

"Follow the river."

"The river?"

"Yes, to a field to a path to a stream. It's very simple really."

"Doesn't sound like it. Not with this smoke and this catastrophe unfolding," Azzie scoffed.

I could still taste the burnt metal in the air. I could see with my two eyes how the smoke lingered. What would this mean for Celia? "It can't be good for you to be out there."

"I don't need help. I mean, really."

The screen flickered into a hot pink and gray pixelation; the room was blinking.

"I must leave and no one can know. Two is too many."

"I don't want you to," Azzie said, "but I can't stop you."

Celia seemed relieved. She gave Azzie a small scrap of paper with a series of numbers written on it. She said, "There are ways you can help, supplies you can gather. Also, find a map with these coordinates." She said she needed warm clothes in dark shades, a kerchief and hiking boots and a lighter. Food too. Dry goods.

"And a scarf and mask to breathe through," I added. "I don't get why this nurse is so secretive."

"Don't you know how dangerous it is to resist?" She looked surprised, like I should know.

"Resist what?"

"Valedictorian. Supplements. Lumena Corp."

"Lumena? What do you mean?"

"Not taking only endangers yourself," Azzie said. We'd heard this repeated.

"Says Dr. Billy. There are other dangers too," Celia said. I guess she was proof of this. "The fears people don't have words for are the ones that haunt. There's another name for the group, I'm not sure what it is but they call themselves *resistors*."

I searched for this in the database. I came up with limited hits, mainly index pages. Even then, the pages were filled with mostly white space. I read aloud from a selection:

"A loose network of ecologically minded feminists, who've chosen to live without augmentation. Against systemically enforced chemical maintenance. Known to gather and form temporary camps for short durations, weeks or months, then disperse. Many spend only part of their

time on the periphery. They don't fully remove themselves from augmented communities. Believe this to be a more effective strategy. A surprising majority were trained as medical professionals before turning against the pharmaco-industrial complex."

And another:

"—illicit activities include drug smuggling, sex rituals, human trafficking. They are suspected in multiple kidnappings and disappearances. Past and current charges include obstruction of chemical delivery, kidnapping, personal endangerment, and a refusal to pay licensing fees. They often lead double lives and are determined to destroy the social fabric."

Azzie was wide-eyed. "WUT?! Is that true?"

"Not all of it. Many things are said about them."

"Then why haven't we heard of them?!"

I kept reading:

"... refer to themselves individually as 'resistors'—the name comes from the electrical circuit: A resistor reduces current flow and lowers voltage within a circuit. Reduce the current. Reduce reliance on augmentation. Take back from the factory, its reserves. Upset the balance, disrupt the hoarding of profits and resources that belong to us all."

"That's it?" Azzie said.

"The gist."

"Celia, this doesn't sound safe."

"I just know what Jai told me. About the possibility of living without augmentation. Of creating a commons. Of forging a space of presence and attention. Without screens. Wandering and wondering as a way of being."

"So you'd give up your antler and all, and leave us to go with them?"

"I don't want to take anything produced by the factory."

I was shocked. "Ok, then," I said, rolling my eyes toward Azzie—was this what happened with Erasure? Who was Celia without supplements? I mean who were any of us, really?

XXII.

Celia asked us for a device to use. I pulled mine out and offered it to her. She hesitated. Scrutinized the case. "Is anyone monitoring this?"

"I don't think?"

"Not Judy? You have to be sure."

"Look, you can use mine," Azzie said. "I'm sure Trinie hasn't touched it." She shoved the device toward Celia and then walked into the next room.

I followed her out and shut the door. Her back was to me. She was looking out the window.

I reached into my pocket, pulled out a small red-and-purple pill-shaped case, opened it and tapped it on my palm. Took a green halfmoon. AnzietEZ. Bit it. Held out the other half to Azzie.

"This is messing with me," she said.

"We've all had too much mindfuck even before this." I nodded back to the other room.

"Celia's erratic, and then you—"

"I'm fine. I mean, I will be. Your mother said." She was the one adult I trusted.

I knew Azzie wouldn't mention what I assumed she was thinking about but would never say: traveling beyond Lumena, her father and his disappearance. She never talked about him, ever. Mentioning any part of it was like turning a switch. She'd stop talking. Leave the room. He'd been a transporter for Lumena, drove truckloads of raw materials from their point of arrival to the factory, and then left the factory with truckloads of supplements to be distributed. His coming and going was normal, but one day he'd left. He never returned. I had imagined many nightmarish scenarios that he'd encountered out there. It wasn't hard to. *Anything could happen*, they said, beyond the perimeter. It was dangerous. No one ever explained why. I'd just always known this.

Azzie and I sat on the floor, dimmed the lights. Our screens were bright. She took out the scrap of paper Celia had given her and typed in coordinates. I then traced the route from the factory and into the forest. We tried to track a path to the camp but there wasn't any way to tell what she'd find other than trees.

Still, we printed aerial maps on vinyl sheets. We made notes on them, too, but I wasn't convinced it would help. I started to make a list of what we'd need—water, bug spray, these maps, a padded mat, masks, bolt cutters, walking shoes, a few days of supplements.

Jai responded to Celia's text within the hour. Celia came in, sat on the floor beside us, and gave Azzie her phone back. Told us of her communications, then showed us the message:

glad to hear yr on the other side. instructions will follow.

will be waiting for you. J

1. you have been given the route. do not deviate. do not write it, leave no traces.
2. come alone. tell no one.
3. turn off gps/location services/wireless. remove your data chip. use mnemonic devices if you have difficulty remembering.
4. leave in darkness.
5. wear dark clothes, cover skin: pants, sleeves, scarf. bring hiking boots and hydration. a flashlight/flares. energy pacs. night vision if you have access.

reply with "affirmative" if you understand. text again when you depart but not again. we will be waiting.

Azzie showed Celia the route we'd traced and argued for the impossibility of her finding her way on her own through the forest and brush. "If you're going then I'm going too," she insisted.

"I'm going alone," Celia said.

"You say so but..."

"No but's. Jai was clear. She's very strict about these things."

"It's too dangerous, especially with the smoke and toxicities. Let the air clear at least."

"Two fools are no wiser than one."

"Can't you ask?" I interjected. "Can't we come part of the way?"

"No communications. I must follow instructions."

"And where was she when you left the hospital?" Azzie pointed out. "If I hadn't found you, then what—"

"I would've made do. Remember I called you. I didn't have to. Look, I've already messaged. I must be on my way before dawn."

We must go with you, we insisted.

"We must go as three," I said.

Azzie turned to me. "Don't you even start. Remember, I'm looking after you." She said I was to stay here and rest. Trinie's orders, and now hers too.

"Because my mind might be falling? If so, I say bring it." I refused to conjure what this could lead to. I couldn't face the two of them leaving without me. *My mare, we must share*, was my new mantra, I decided then and there. "I'm coming too and there's nothing you can do about it."

Celia yelled, "Look, you both need to stop or I'm leaving right now. Force quit. That's it."

Azzie responded, "Fuck both of you." And she didn't use fuck like I used fuck so I knew she wasn't fucking around.

We all stood there in silence, agitated and glaring at each other, in this dim, dark room.

"So what time do I set the alarm for?" It was

obvious who Azzie was asking.

"Sunrise is at what time?" Celia asked.

"Five-ten."

"Then set it for quarter to."

That was it, no further discussion. Azzie set the alarm and we all went to bed.

[PACKING LIST]

Ener-G bars and HiKal pacs
black hood and scarf, pants and boots (x 3)
sleeping mats
a lighter
industrial flashlights
a laser pointer
a Swiss army knife (*Azzie's father's*)
a 3D-printed sundial
maps with the route traced
coordinates, compass (analog)
rehydration powder & e-lyte+ water (2)
pills. plenty: Delixir, AnzietEZ, eBoost and V.

XXIII. OFF-LABEL USE

We dressed in black—boots, pants and bomber jackets—tucked our hair under our hats, covered our faces with scarves. Soot was everywhere and the smoke was denser and darker than any kind we were used to. It looked like embers of the fire were still burning. We walked over the bridge to Factory Hill, then climbed over a series of fences.

The top of the hill was now like a crater filled with smoke and sky. In the factory's place were twisted metal frames and the remains of charred walls.

This was the type of disaster I'd only seen in photos: grass yellowed, trees stripped of leaves, soot adrift.

Celia stopped. Said she saw men in suits hiding behind the trees, phalanxes of them moving in. "Too late, too late," she mumbled. I tried to assure her the men were only in her mind. She didn't look so sure, but we kept on regardless.

On the back side of the hill: a swarm of tents, set up in rows amid so much soot and detritus. They were low to the ground like webbed tunnels. Azzie walked toward them.

"Never wake the sleeping bear," Celia warned.

I wondered what these tents were doing here but I

agreed we had a purpose. It was better to not risk any encounters.

Azzie didn't care. She ran up to the closest tent lifted a flap, then disappeared. She stepped out and motioned for us to come.

A few seconds later, Celia said she heard someone calling. I heard no one; I looked around and saw no one. Before I could respond, Celia took off toward the tree line. I ran after her hoping Azzie would see us and follow.

I had expected there to be some kind of physical boundary between us and the beyond—chicken wire or a series of signs that say Do Not Enter or a wall, a series of surveillance cameras, an electric fence? Maybe there was something that I couldn't see but mostly it seemed like we were entering a forest. One side of the boundary looked just like the other. How was there nothing to mark this when it was so pronounced in my mind? There are physical boundaries like rivers and mountains, and ones that humans build to control the flow of people—to keep some out and to keep others from leaving. But none was here.

We paused for Azzie to catch up. Celia gave her a peevish look. Azzie, between gasps, tried to reassure Celia that no one was on the hill or in the tents, though she said that what was within the tents was curious. Celia said it would be silly to think there wasn't anyone there, but we had no time to discuss this.

"We must move swiftly," Celia said, "and you follow my lead or you leave." Azzie conceded she would do this, and then Celia instructed us to remove the chips from our devices.

We kept on through the shadows. *Nothing but trees*, Judy was right about that. I felt dizzied by the seeming endlessness of these trees and their branches, the tangled paths of vines and leaves that lay between them. Removed from the constant waves of information, I felt something new. A sense of nothingness. A forest full.

I had thought once we were out here we'd hear birds calling, crickets chirping, and I'd be swatting off insects, but there was no sign of life other than the trees. I stood at the base of one—its trunk rose for a hundred feet before its branches sprawled out, reaching to the others around it. Its leaves were still green. This was good. At least the air seemed to be clearing.

"I keep thinking about how easy it is to disappear," Azzie stated after a long lull. I wondered if she feared her own desire to hide. I didn't say this but liked this idea of disappearing. Anything felt possible now that we were out here.

If anything, I felt more present. I also felt kind of bored. Perhaps this was ennui? I'd never felt it before. I was in awe of how far the land stretched and its monotony. And we hadn't traveled that far even—a few kilometers, maybe. I wondered how the resistors recognized each other. It was easier out here, I guessed.

We saw a stream in the distance. It had been a point on the map. Its appearance seemed to say, *welcome you are finding your way.*

"Good, good," Celia muttered under her breath. She suggested we take a second to recalibrate.

In the light the water reflected a dreamy sea green that swirled into pale pink. When I stood over the water I could see below. There were so many fish that if I had a net I could catch twenty with one sweep. This didn't seem right. It looked like we could walk across their silver backs and white bellies to the other side. I panicked. I thought of the fires in Lumena, the chemicals released—were they making a mad dash to flee?

"Oh brainfuck! Come look."

Azzie ran up beside me and stared at the fish. "Do you think?" she asked. Then paused. If fish could stampede this is surely what was happening.

"Oh dear, oh no," Celia said when she saw.

I sighed and shook my head, "These poor fish."

"Not a good day to take a swim," Azzie said.

"Not funny," I said. But I understood her sentiment. There was no use standing here watching them flee when we could do nothing. There was no point in lamenting. "Maybe it's better downstream."

As we followed the stream there were fewer fish.

We kept on and my mind kept drifting back to an outline of Tigue pointing to the factory as if issuing a warning. This somehow came back with a ferocity. I stumbled a bit. I must have been talking out loud because Azzie was talking at me.

"Jeni would've mentioned something, you know, if Tigue had beef with the factory." Jeni had worked closely with Tigue but I wasn't so sure she would've known this.

"It seems superstitious..." Celia said.

Celia was not one to speak. *Superstitious* was a better word for Celia's mother's belief system that had no one defining characteristic other than many desperate attempts to find threads of meaning. Celia's mother double- and triple- dipped into Buddhas and holy water, pagan holidays, prayer, meditation, altars to familial spirits, voodoo. She had once told Celia that invisible forces directed our lives and she could influence them with her clear energy. But I was with Shelley on this. He was a staunch atheist. "Poets are the unacknowledged legislators," he'd written. I knew no poets either but I wished I did.

"I sense her more here, somehow. I don't know why."

"Maybe your treatment wasn't complete?" Azzie suggested. Azzie, always swifter to greet the obvious. She was a fan of Occam's razor. In fact she was the one who'd made me aware of this name for the theory that the most direct explanation is often the most plausible. And yet when I'd heard this, I just wondered who this man Occam was and what else he'd cut beyond the shortest line between cause and effect.

I didn't need anyone to agree with me. If Tigue was directing me I would eventually uncover something. I decided not to say anything more. I didn't ask Celia what chemicals coaxed her mother's epiphanies. I didn't need anyone to believe that I could still see Tigue's gaze and that her hand was pointing in the direction we were headed.

There was so much beyond our knowing. Not that these were *reasons* per se. That's magical thinking. But I did believe there were interconnections and occurrences and causes and effects beyond our awareness.

We had walked so far it seemed entirely possible that we'd find the chimps playing in the next clearing. Or tucked away in a pocket of trees. But there weren't any. No bears or badgers, no wildcats, no hares. Whatever wildness out here had fled. I looked up and imagined a million tiny cameras in the sky. I started to feel dizzy. Then I saw a flash, then many, like paparazzi.

The woods, the trees, Azzie and Celia and the sun before me, came into focus and then disappeared.

Then I was staring at the sky. Azzie and Celia stood over me, making me sip from a cup, picking something off my body.

When I looked up again their faces had transformed. Their mouths had widened and grown forward. They had hair sprouting everywhere. I closed my eyes—this couldn't be. Soon they were handling me; I felt hands on my body and like I was swinging in the air. Then I heard a cooing in my ear, telling me not to think.

My body tingled. My mind was pins and needles. I tried to describe—

My mouth made shapes but I made no sound.

Their faces looked warped with jagged lines framing the edges.

"Shhh shhh," Azzie said to me. "Just rest."

I felt shame. I couldn't think of why.

Celia said, "Mind misshooting." Azzie said, "Pineapple rotting."

I heard a third voice I didn't recognize.

"Hush, don't talk—" I was told.

After a minute, or was it an hour?, I could feel my mind coming together.

"We'll wait here until you recover from this spell," the voice assured me.

We, who? She was not we.

Azzie pushed my hair back and whispered to me: "She seems okay, I think? She appeared from nowhere."

They helped me into the shade.

"The chimps..." I thought of their faces. I managed to mutter this at some point.

Celia shook her head like she had no idea what I meant.

A woman stood over me in her big brown boots. She had thick legs and a lithe frame. She held a bottle of water up to my mouth. I moved my mask. She placed a pill on my palm. "A relaxant," she said, "— you left us for a moment."

"It was no rapture." Azzie sounded like she was on edge.

Celia frowned. Her mother had an old, peeling bumper sticker that warned that, in the event of, *this car will be unmanned.*

"It's a metaphor," the woman said.

"I have no time for word games," Celia protested.

"I'm not here for games."

I had to think through so many words. Each phrase running on a loop before my mouth followed suit. "Who...are you?" I eventually spat out.

My mouth felt like it was full of rocks, not good to chew.

She said we could call her Jules. She'd been looking

for signs of chemical seepage. She saw us wandering and figured we must be lost.

"You should take a look at that stream back there," Azzie said, gesturing behind us.

The woman nodded. "Yes, I know."

"Well we aren't lost."

"I gather you're not out here for pleasure."

"And we don't need your help—we have permits," Azzie lied. "And these." She lifted her scarf to reveal her mask.

"The air and water are tainted. I wouldn't be out here today if I had my druthers." This woman seemed serious. I wondered what we'd have to do to get away if she didn't believe us.

Celia started scratching again. She did this now when she was restless. She stood up quickly, grabbed her pack. "Anyway, whatever. I'm sorry you all, but I've got to run."

"In which direction?" asked Jules. Her interest seemed piqued.

"Can't say!"

"What if I said, I think I know the way?"

"It isn't the plan. Really, must fly now. Byyyye!" She picked up her bag quickly and turned away.

"And if I have directions?" Jules called out.

Celia hesitated, then stopped. "Say more."

I didn't believe some woman was waiting here without design. It was impossible, really. I couldn't bring myself to think of how, but she was pointing to the same things we were pointing to—coordinates, a circuitous path. She seemed to sidestep our questions to redirect them to her own interest.

"I've received instructions." She looked at Celia. "I believe you have, too."

"I was told 'no deviations.'"

"I was told you would come alone."

Celia's face puckered.

"I understand your concern, but don't be stupid."

This was true. It seemed obvious. Celia reluctantly agreed to follow Jules for a while, but at a distance.

Out here the trees looked taller than the tallest buildings I've seen. I don't recall much else. Just a seemingly endless path before spotting a house at the top of the hill, walking up a long gravel drive, and at the top, finding a trailer, too, and a covered shelter beside it.

I remember a dog barking like it wanted at us. And a tall woman struggling to hold him back.

I remember entering the trailer and Jules leading me to a couch. I closed my eyes and when I opened them the sun was still out.

Did it ever go down? It felt like we'd spent days in the forest.

The tall woman was now sitting with her back to me.

Her hair was mousy. She wore overalls.

I sat up. Azzie and Celia weren't here. I tried to lift myself from the couch.

The woman heard me rustling and turned around. "Been wondering how long you'd be out. Don't worry, your friends are out back."

I turned and looked out the window behind me and saw a big patch of dirt and a wolf dog at its edge. He was now tethered to a tree, still barking.

"Don't mind him," the woman said. "He's not used to so much activity."

I didn't see any sign of Azzie or Celia. I didn't understand how Azzie left me alone with this woman when she was supposed to be looking after me.

"...so you *live* here?"

"Sure. I work with trees. I have for a long time. I don't need much company."

Although she wasn't saying anything difficult, I still had a hard time engaging. I needed to sit and balance my head. Every breath required a certain amount of concentration.

She walked to the other side of the room to a stove where she lit a match and transferred the flame to a burner. She warmed a kettle, then brought over a mug of hot water with a sachet of plant material steeping.

"Looks like grass," I said.

"A tincture to clear your head." She explained that

it was actually natural. She'd picked some nettles just earlier today.

I thanked her and set the drink aside.

She was still standing over me, I'm not sure why. I didn't want to take a sip but I did. And then I took another.

A few minutes later I felt looser, more like myself.

Had she told me her name? I couldn't remember. I asked. She said to call her Marj. And what was she doing? She said "routing."

"What's that?"

She ignored me for a while and remained focused on the paper. So quaint. It was spread across the desk with a few books on each side, and pens spread out around them.

There were screens in windows, made of small wires forming small rectangles. "These keep the bugs out?"

The woman uh-huhed at me, not taking her eyes off what she was doing.

My extinction list didn't include insects, bugs, or arachnids either. There were too many to keep track of and their big buggy eyes and wings freaked me out. They deserved to live too, but I was glad for the screens. There were lamps but they looked old-timey like Harold's old brassy kerosene lamp stored in the basement with his boxes. We had tried to use it once, when the power went out, but its fuel had long ago turned to muck.

"Do you have electricity?"

She shook her head. "Off the grid. We got a few generators."

I told her I'd never spent a night beyond the perimeter. There were Judy's spa weekends and resort trips but these places had their own clear boundaries. Nothing like this.

"You live like animals do," I told her.

"You know, we're all animals."

"Yes, but...we're evolved." I hesitated. "I mean us humans." As soon as I uttered this I wanted to take it back. I didn't believe it really, though I'd heard it so many times that it was the first thing that came to mind. I figured it's what she'd want to hear.

"If you're talking about learning to repress, perhaps—"

That was not the answer I expected even if she was an adult who drew out plans on paper. I lay back on the couch again, and closed my eyes and wondered, what did she mean by *repress*?! Hadn't I thought this, in my own way while observing the chimps' tenderness, wishing for some of it, only to be told I was wrong? Hadn't Judy been weary when I started monitoring the extinction list, wondering at what point we'd fall onto it? Hadn't I been told I couldn't live with the chimps precisely because they lived in nature and learned by instinct? We had different needs

213

and our livelihoods relied on advancing technology.

When I'd asked why we cared more about our own propagation than our planet's, Judy had reprimanded me, said "propagation" was a very detached word. I didn't care. I didn't want to become a mother because children were annoying—not to mention a drain on the planet.

I had wanted to escape more than anything. Escape Lumena, escape the civilized world, escape our dying planet. I'd wondered how many other planets in our universe held life forms and if their forms were more intelligent than ours. Judy didn't care about animals. Her decision to eat only plant-based foods was an excuse to eat like a bird. *Pencil thin is win, win!* would have been Judy's mantra if she had one.

The dog started howling again. I recalled its piercing teeth. Marj walked to the screen and yelled back at him. Her tone softened. "She's just waking up," I heard her say.

She turned to me and said my friends were going down to the mulch piles, did I want to go too?

I sat up and saw Azzie and Celia by a shed with a wheelbarrow. This seemed so improbable. I wanted to laugh.

Marj told me to freshen up and throw some water on my face. I somehow managed to stand. The washroom was cramped, with plastic fixtures and running water. The water on my face felt so fresh.

I ambled into the musky room and out the door, and as I walked away Marj yelled, "Don't let her do any heavy lifting—you hear?"

XXIV. BROUGHT TO YOU BY LUMENA CORP.

On the drive to the storage site, Judy had time to think. The smoke was heavier and thicker than she'd ever seen. She saw soot drifts piled against buildings, scattered across cars and lawns, dirtying everything. She wore a scarf over her N95 mask and had another in her purse. Hannah, master of indirect discourse, hadn't called, hadn't responded at all to her messages. It was Harold, gaped mouth, staring at the screen who informed her that their daughter was staying at Azzie's. Maybe it was for the better. Everyone but essential workers were advised to remain indoors for the next twenty-four. As head of the Learning Committee she was essential. Of the essence, she thought. That she had work ahead was calming, though what was distressing were her thoughts of Hannah and her pineapple mind sliding.

The school stockpile was stored at the local PRPL HILLS LIFE STORAGE. She parked in the mostly empty lot and walked to the entrance. The building took up the entire block and looked like a box. She punched in her key code and the gate opened to a dark hallway. At unit #218 she punched in another code. The gate lifted slowly. Dr. Billy stood behind it in his brilliant white coat. He stood before towers of boxes, lining the walls, filling the room, leaving only a narrow path to walk through.

"You'll find the inventory for each unit by the door." Billy pointed to the clipboard hanging on the wall.

Judy examined the list, "Yes, of course. And so far?"

"I estimate we have 500,000 doses. That doesn't include topicals and injection—" He was collected, despite the heightened anxiety. One thing she admired about Billy was his presence, though she never could get a good read of what was below the surface.

"Yes, of course." She leaned against a stack of boxes. "This is all so unsettling."

"And Hannah?" he asked, "how is she?"

"I suspect—" Hannah's name, still a rock in her stomach. "I haven't seen her since yesterday, before your appointment."

Judy felt Billy's hand on her shoulder. "She has so much potential and yet..."

"She rejects it! And now..."

His fingers started kneading her knotty back. "She will come around, I believe."

"Yes, we'll see. I appreciate that you've been here for me." He was her ally—maybe her only? Harold only ever responded to her concerns with a blank gaze.

She looked back to the list on the wall. *Focus*, she

thought. "The students will thank you," she said. She straightened her dress and shut out her worry and whatever warmth she felt.

"Let's get to it." He held out his palm holding two bright red capsules, one for each of them.

Focal Point keeps eyes steady, on target.

Focal Point keeps eyes steady, on target.

cal Point keeps eyes steady, on target.

With clipboard in hand, Judy counted the number of capsules contained within bottles packed within boxes. Hour after hour, she walked through the stacks, taking meticulous notes. The evening turned to night in these musty rooms, as they eased around corners, their bodies passing in close quarters. Tallies for each unit were posted just inside each gate.

Judy thought only in numbers. Billy stood before her counting and she felt his authority as if it were a calming energy. She could almost see it, the color of a warm sun. Visualizing this helped calm her too.

The amount of VALEDICTORIAN on hand, including bulk powders, might be all they needed to power their children's minds until the factory could regroup. They would have to be meticulous. She also made sure to set one box to the side. Surely no one would notice, and if they did surely they wouldn't blame her for this small indemnity. She placed the box below Billy's desk and moved on to her next task.

Later, much, they held a planning session under lamplight, surrounded by lists of student names and weights and regimens, a two-year calendar and a list of doses in each unit. After drafting plans for school-aged children, they'd see how much they'd have to give to others in the community. Would they need to ration? It was likely.

She and Billy met with four other committee members who had assisted in counting. All six of them beleaguered by the draft and dim lights. She had so many numbers running through her head: with six thousand children of eligible age, with dosing based on weight and taken three times a day, the average child weighing less than an adult (thank goodness!), with a stockpile of a hundred thousand capsules, how long would it last?

By the time night ceded to the small hours it was just Judy and Billy left, still hunched over the desk, their yawning contagious. Billy placed his palm on her back, then her thigh. She welcomed it. The night unfurled: he unzipped himself and she braced atop the desk and fell into breath, losing her sense of the oh and all.

Afterward in the cramped bathroom, she coifed her hair. She had not expected this. Though in retrospect it seemed inevitable. Long day, late night. Seduced by bad light and close quarters. And that box, of course. Not that Billy would've blinked an eye. They made a good team, mostly. It'd been right there below them the entire time and he'd made no mention of it. As if it were invisible. She'd just fixed her skirt, picked up the box and walked out. She wondered what four steps she should take next.

Billy offered to walk her to her car. She said it was unnecessary. He said he needed air and followed her through the sliding doors into the lot. The sky was still dark, the floodlights illuminated flies buzzing and soot still soft in the air. She paused halfway to the car, placed the box on the ground while pretending to look for her keys. She looked up and for the first time she saw a discernible sadness on his face, or so she thought—it was hard to see. He stood aside as she opened the car door and he continued to stand there as she drove off, until he became a pinpoint in the distance.

XXV. REBOUND ANXIETY

Harold reeled at the thought of an air bubble rippling through the make-up of the universe like an air bubble in an IV line. It could be headed toward them at this moment and they'd never know until it hit. He knew this was paranoid and yet he'd heard something of this, too, in his streams. All of the disaster talk. It was within the realm of possibilities. This was what it felt like, because how else would he have explained this utter state of disconnect, not even Hannah or Judy with him. No one would've had the foresight to see the disruption of one tiny particle upending time. Not a butterfly but one tiny chemical amplified, multitudes of pills, a river flowing, coursing through veins, activating—and then nothing. And then backorder.

Fear was the first feeling Harold had felt in so long. Empathy wasn't on backorder. But he needed to secure a month's supply. At least, in case they became hard to find. Only four weeks in, and now: flits of feeling descended every so often. He felt electric shocks up his arms. And! His words weren't always absconding, not anymore.

When he arrived at the dispensary, he saw a line of bodies from the counter, wrapping around aisles, circling the perimeter, then forming a tail out the door. So much circumference to this line. Circles within circles. Twenty minutes passed, one foot forward. The man ahead of him turned around and offered a stick of gum at hour one. Harold declined. At hour two he passed through the digital technologies aisle, had access to meters that measure blood flow, inspiration, potential oxygenation, synaptic currents. He placed his arm in a glove that measured his pressures and such:

Too hot! Too fat! Mental state: At Capacity!

By hour three, the man standing in front of him had developed sweat circles radiating from his pits. Harold saw the diameter expanding, wondered at what rate. Given enough time the circles would meet and wrap around this man's body.

He checked his device. No calls, no messages. Hannah, where was she? In the next aisle, two women fought over the last bundle of toilet paper until a security officer wedged himself between. By the time all was settled Harold was fourth in line. He could then see behind the counter: white shelves tall and empty, bottles scattered. He could almost see a cloud above the counter from the pills and powders shifting from one container to another. The four faces behind the counter were pale and cold.

Well, they certainly aren't on Empathy, he thought, *maybe there will be some left for me!*

"Harold Marcus!" The voice behind the counter called. He walked up. Another white coat was holding a bag.

"Lucky man, you've got the last of our Empathy," the woman said, placing a bag on the counter. "We only have twelve. Partial fill."

How could that be?!

"You can pay out of pocket if you want these. Insurance isn't approving any advances. I'd recommend it. With all this ruckus, stock's depleted. I get more in and it's gone. Pay now and you can pick up what you're owed after our next delivery arrives."

He didn't trust this assurance. He'd seen notice of the backorder splashed across his screens. He'd waited in this line. And this woman, she was wearing scrubs covered with little cats wearing pajamas. He found these cats confounding but comforting. He decided he would not find this woman trustworthy enough to do something like heart surgery, but he would take her comfort and swallow the empathy if she handed him a pill.

"I need twenty—at least. I've been waiting for hours! Please."

She shook her head. She said she had emptied her last container. Did she have to show him this?

He looked behind him to see the line now longer

than when he'd started. He shook his head no. He gave her his card and she gave him the bag and completed the transaction.

Harold spent the rest of the evening at home, with lights on and news streaming all of this unrest. He gazed at fire dancing across the screen, saw images of Judy too, with Billy—they were securing stockpiles, said the news. What were they doing other than telling him what he already knew? It was irritating, ingratiating. He wondered why Judy still wasn't by his side. Why hadn't Hannah messaged to update him? Only texts from Azzie saying Hannah was spending the night. He sat on the sofa all night, gazing at the screen, alone with his worry.

"It's just the beginning," said the newscaster on the nightly news.

The camera zoomed in on two correspondents, their eyes with dark circles: "Respiratory distress has subsided, with no additional casualties. There is hope and yet the backorder will be detrimental. Will Valedictorian be rationed? Will minds fall and fail? This might be the scourge of a generation."

Behind the women: twisted beams and fire smoldering.

On screen: bodies draped in white, heads, hands and

feet covered, walking through fields in misshapen lines, bending, picking up shards and warped metal, placing them in bags.

Regarding the shortage, Dr. Billy speaks. "No need to worry about an interruption in VALEDICTORIAN's supply line," he said. He forced a smile. "We have stockpiles. We'll get through this."

Lines at dispensaries tumbled out of doors, supplies were exhausted, depleted of supplements, of VALE-DICTORIAN, of bottles of MangaKWIK, which had been touted as a cure-all for the heaves.

Word of mouth spread, or rather, moved from mouth to ear to finger to screen, was amplified digitally, exponentially. Someone was to blame. A shadow, a group, women wearing masks, carrying axes? Who'd ever envisioned such things?

On the news, interviews: "I saw the bodies moving swiftly, almost inconspicuously. Like ants in a line, working under a chain of command."

The past burns into a fallow future. So many chemicals had trickled into the river, so many were burned and inhaled.

MangaKWIK, a special formulation of Albanian manganese modified for immediate release, to amplify immune system functioning and as a preventive for respiratory disease: add two teaspoons to 8 ounces of water and drink.

XXVI. RESULTING FROM DISCONTINUATION

Dr. Billy hadn't slept since the fires started. Two days in, he maintained his cognitive patency with VIGI-Lante, placed two strips below his tongue every six hours as needed—and when he did he'd feel a jolt run through his spine. Two days seemed like a lifetime. This was a setback, he reasoned but not in the long run.

From his fifth-story office suite it looked like Lumena's citizens had one of three destinations: the base of Factory Hill to witness the destruction for themselves, the dispensary counters, and the petting zoo. Incongruous but true. Perhaps cuteness was also a cure-all. He made note. Even people without the heaves were not in their right mind. People were gathering by the river's edge, as if they wanted to cross over to witness what had burned-out. Now that soot had settled and some advisories had been lifted, it's as if people were drawn to the site of the wound like platelets congregating. It was like a mass hypnosis.

He'd heard reports of one-click buying limits reached, servers at capacity, credit limits exceeded. There was a run on lithium batteries and portable chargers, dosing kits and purified water. Not to mention anxiolytics, soporifics, and all kinds of feel good, pleasure-filled pills. VALEDICTORIAN was being rationed but all of the dispensaries in the town had already run out.

The phone rang all morning. He silenced his calls for the afternoon. Needed to see what he could discern from the medical literature. The symmetry of events was disconcerting.

From the information before him he developed a few hypotheses:

Chemical release from the fire causing residual effects. In this case, those closer to the fire should exhibit more severe symptoms. From the data that had been gathered, this was unlikely.

A mass hysterical response. Somatic symptoms surface in sympathy with those suffering respiratory distress, reflecting deep-seated anxiety, fear of death and insentience. For further investigation: the mysterious Kazakh sleeping sickness, where children would fall asleep in class, curl up in the middle of the street and sleep for days. Some even wandered the streets in this unconscious state. It was similar and yet.

Withdrawal. Given the recommendation for lowering doses of V. during the emergency and the depletion, this was possible though it was too soon to be widespread. He'd seen it before on a case-by-case basis. Lowering doses of V. affected cognitive abilities, across all ages. Usually this was a transient state, though individual experiences were difficult to predict. People reported all sorts of things.

In the health department office all screens streamed different chatter. Judy preferred to watch the news anchors who wore tank tops under tight fitting jackets, with makeup thick, hair rounded. They were paired in twos and threes, and when not talking their glances imparted warmth, as if they were looking directly at her.

They talked over clips showing crews in hazmat suits walking over the burn-out on Factory Hill. Then the camera panned to the hospital overflow and they spoke of patients with breathing problems—still no response in serious cases.

Just beyond Judy's window, protestors gathered with signs written in marker.

She was placing the final touches on her latest permutation of her four steps: Four Steps for Emergency Situations. *Four plus four is magic*, she thought. What if it helped calm the unrest? Why did people not have faith in their leadership? Why did she feel so anxious? The fear needed to be accommodated, domesticated, even, before more damage occurred.

Billy had requested she deliver a talk to address this all that evening. She would try to harness the anger of the factory workers, the domestic servants, the environmental service workers, the mothers out there with all their concern, and she would attempt to redirect it. "The key is to encourage taking positive action," Billy had said. "They need to believe the situation isn't dire. I know you have the ability to do this."

She'd agreed. "The primal response is to act out or shut down. They need assurances."

"We all do."

"Something tells me you don't." She couldn't quite understand how.

"I do have confidence we'll get through this."

She understood this, but to hear him say it was maddening. Sometimes he was so overly smug. "Yes, I see that. I feel I'm a conduit for you."

He nodded. "Yes, conduits—women generally are."

She smiled and nodded, then began to resent that she did. She began to hate him even, for his dismissal of what she was contributing. And her own hasty bargaining. A weight began to fester in her chest.

For a moment she envisioned their roles in a system, she the conduit, like an aqueduct, set in place for transit between one location and another. Billy was the self-appointed engineer, monitoring and adjusting water levels, in control.

She admired the engineer but thought the conduit was just as important if not more so. Besides, any one piece wasn't as important as the entire system working together.

An aqueduct has use too, she thought, even after Billy left the room. Better than being a dry field in a drought. She served the farmers of the world—not farmers per se, but her services assisted the cultivation of minds by helping them grow and mature. *Her role was important too*, she thought. She heard the generators start to whir, their drone drowning out the voices of the television news while the noise in her mind amplified.

TABLE 5: ADVERSE REACTIONS REPORTED BY >1% OF VALEDICTORIAN USERS

System/Organ Class	Valedictorian	Placebo
Neurological Networks/Nervous System		
disconnect, disorientation, amnesia, disassociation, in withdrawal but not limited to	11%	7%
spatial awareness dimming, muddying of mental agility, inability to story-tell or process incoming information, in general, moving to lower states of awareness erratically, indefinitely	4-9%	5%
hallucinations, delusions, an increased reliance on (weak) intuitive states	2%	0.112%
dream state while awake, feeling of slipping away, seeing gray, "sleepwalking" intermittent/ inconsistent processing	4.5%	0.1%

blister, bruise, an undoing of connective tissues	3%	0%
Musculoskeletal disorders		
weakness of muscles, arms, and legs, perceiving an exaggerated delay between thought and action	17%	10%
lethargy and the like	2%	7%
lethargy and the like with abrupt discontinuation (refractory)	26%	13%

XXVIII. DISHABITUATION and SENSITIZATION

I emerged from the trailer into the bright afternoon light. With the crunch of dirt and leaves below my feet and the trees in their multitudes surrounding me, I had the sense of waking from a deep sleep. And yet the sun was the same place as it was when we'd arrived.

"Hey you," Azzie yelled out when she saw me. She ran up the hill toward me and when she was closer, she said, "I was worried that it might be worse...a repeat of, you know."

"I don't. I'd just appreciate you not leaving me in some stranger's house if I happen to pass out again."

"Celia and I went to check on you a few times but she wouldn't let us in. She said you needed to rest."

I thought of Trinie telling me to lock myself in a closet and I'd done the opposite. Kind of.

"She gave me some nettle tea that helped restore me."

"Sure, the tea and, like, twenty-four hours of sleep."

"Stop it."

"You were out for an entire day. I just wanted to make sure you were still breathing but Marj wouldn't have it."

I had no sense of all that time having passed or where I was within it.

Azzie led me down the hill to the mulch piles. Celia welcomed me as she threw a shovelful into the barrow. She said she wanted to hug me but she was so gross and sweaty. They'd been redistributing the mulch over the fields and footpaths. They were supposed to harvest what looked ripe and to uproot and turn whatever else back into the soil. They had said they didn't know what ripe looked like—we'd never worked with dirt—but they were told to do what they could. And we were welcome to pick and eat whatever if we were hungry.

The mulch piles looked like mounds of shredded trees. Celia sat down at one's base and started scratching her legs. She had her hair up in a topknot, with sweat wetting her baby hair and plastering it to her cheeks. Azzie wore her hair back in a kerchief. She picked up a shovel and started taking shovelfuls from the mound and dumping them into the wheelbarrow.

"They're leaving tomorrow," Celia said. "The woman who told us to mulch said they've got to 'scatter.'"

"Leaving for where?"

"I don't know. I don't think the where matters."

"We spent last night in a cabin," Azzie added, "made from trees they'd downed themselves. Breakfast this morning was fried eggs and grits."

"Jules said someone dropped off the eggs before we woke."

"There's hens?" I suddenly felt like I'd missed out on all the things.

"Nearby, I think," Azzie said. "And they said we could stay tonight if we made ourselves useful."

"Ok, but we need to get back, like yesterday."

"You're in no shape," Azzie said.

"If Trinie comes home and we're not there..." Silence wouldn't cause suspicion, but our absence would.

"We'll come up with some story. Besides, today's Saturday."

If we weren't back for classes that would set off alarms. Celia's disappearance surely already had, but we were likely safe for now as long as no one had connected her absence to ours.

"Ok, but Celia, you're coming with us?"

"Are you kidding, dear? Why would I?"

"Um, your family, your life, and you know, us?"

She looked at me like I was mad.

I looked at Azzie. She'd stopped shoveling and had taken a seat in the wheelbarrow. "Are we okay with Jai?" I asked.

Azzie shrugged. "Haven't met yet."

"But she's here, yes?"

"Yes. I mean, probably," Celia deferred. "I don't know about here-here, at this moment."

"So you haven't seen Jai either."

Celia shook her head no.

"But that was the point of you coming here."

"Her, them, this group. Don't get caught up in semantics, Han."

"This all seems so sus."

"Under what condition would it not?"

"Maybe if we met this person who directed you here but still hasn't bothered to show up."

"It's not like that."

"But—how can you trust their intentions?"

"You sound like my mother. *What's his intention, Celia?*"

"He wants to fuck you, of course," Azzie laughed.

"So that's the vibe you're picking up." She scowled.

"I mean what if they fuck you over. Here we are covering their tracks—I guess? No one's looking out."

"You know what happens if I go home. I mean not *home...*"

"Look, calm down yous," Azzie inserted.

I shut my mouth and closed my eyes and inhaled deeply. The air was crisp, scented with evergreen. After a few moments my head felt clearer.

I opened my eyes. Azzie held a pomegranate in her hands and was cracking it against a rock.

"Where'd you get that?"

"Over there by the gardens." I knew pomegranates grew on trees, but I had no idea what the tree looked like. Only the fruit, its casing and seeds. I found the bright red arils in Azzie's palm alarming.

"No, that's ok. I'm not hungry."

"Jules went back this morning to do more testing," Azzie told me. "Has to do with the factory. She thinks the toxicities might be overreaching."

"Is that why they're leaving?"

Azzie shrugged.

"But wasn't she out there looking for us?—yesterday, I mean."

Celia considered this for a moment. "Not *us*. Don't ask too many questions."

"I mean, I'd just assumed."

"All of this is a blessing," she said. "Don't look too deeply for what you don't need to know. You don't want to be caught like a bear in a trap."

Blessing? Bear in a trap? What was *that* supposed to mean? I thought of her letter and the floorplan of the ward. Was I the bear? Maybe she thought I'd appreciate an animal metaphor.

Out here there were depths, layers. Traces upon traces left by those who were here before. I knew I could barely make sense of them. And if Tigue was still pointing, I was no longer able to tell in which direction. Maybe Azzie was right. Billy had botched my release. But what if—and I'd like to believe this—she had been trying to tell me, tell us, that there's another way to be. A way of thinking about how a life is lived, how you lose yourself, how pills are taken. We'd been told so many things.

I know that the more you think about something that has happened, the more your memory of the event changes. Like, if you recall the same event every day, by the hundredth day you've likely fabricated it in its entirety. The purest memories are the ones left buried. The things never recalled. I hadn't shared all I'd seen with Billy, even though I was unaware of what I'd kept to myself.

It was a message.

A voice in my head.

Like a shriek coming on outside of me. I turned toward the roar and saw a line of four wheelers in the distance. They continued to multiply, as if the women riding had been hiding among the trees. I worried about Celia and her ability to trust—it was one thing I couldn't do, one of many things. No one had her best interest in mind. Best interest is always the best interest of whoever's telling you.

Celia was now staring off in the direction of the four wheelers too. She had this look of anticipation. Soon the four wheelers turned away and were headed back into the trees.

Marj came down and said we needed to go up to the house. We followed her up the dirt path and took off our shoes before entering as requested. Marj led us to a small room with bright lights and various jars scattered on the counter. She introduced us to the nurse, who had a short black bob and pursed lips. The nurse said she wanted to examine Celia first.

Celia removed her shirt and the woman ran her hands over Celia's upper body. She pointed to the indigo bruise on Celia's arm, "When did this start?"

"I don't know...a week ago?" Celia pointed to another on her side. "They come and go."

"Depleted," the nurse said under her breath. "'Spilled ink' is what we call it. Chemical exposure, sensitivities to the environment. Enhancements—all kinds of combinations, two or three or more when taken together, depending. It's likely that the blood's bad. But don't worry," she said to Celia, "it's only dangerous left untreated. Do you know if they were aware of this at the hospital?"

Celia said no one had talked about her treatments except to inform her in the most oblique ways. They had said that she should expect to not feel great. Gave her an electrode for her moods. Some elixir against instability. No one talked to her directly—she was told self-reflection would only make it worse. Celia said all she knew was she had to escape and once she did she would find her way. That birds like her are good with migratory patterns; ancestral memory passes through generations. She knew she had to get out, not the how or why but that she would—the fire was the sign.

This entire account made me squirm. I interrupted, "Okay, but where is Jai anyway?"

"Jai?" The nurse looked surprised.

"Isn't that who Celia's supposed to see?"

Celia glared at me. I wanted answers. I wanted this woman to wonder how much I knew beyond the surface of things.

"Um, well you see, she's caught up in meetings."

I wondered what shape a meeting would take out here. "I mean, really?"

"I know you don't sense anything happens without screens."

"Possibly, but okay?"

"More's happening here than you realize. That's really all I can say." She turned back to Celia, "Your mind will heal but it's hard to know when or in what way. We can help you though."

"But I have never felt more like myself," Celia protested.

"No one ever does. We're all stuck in present tense."

I had wondered the same thing, about feeling myself, except I wasn't exactly sure I knew what that was like. The things I saw always seemed so real in the moment even when they weren't happening—like the chimps appearing, nursing me. Tigue's messages.

Like, would I know my mind was cracking if no one told me? If this is a quantum universe, as Harold insisted again and again without my fully believing him, there was another me sitting in this same house with her mind already gone, and she doesn't even know this.

I wanted to know what was real and what was synthetic, not that I could tell the difference or why it mattered to me. In Lumena we relied on manufactured feelings to make life palatable. Out here it felt different. At home there was a consensus that Lumena was forward-thinking but no one could define this beyond happiness scores and profit margins. We had a right to happiness, to ambition, to be awash in supplements, and to pursue all of the above. We were damned if we didn't.

There was no incentive to care about the state of the planet or the nature of our natures. It was a downer. Better, they'd say, we could find ways to use technology in its place, like watching dolphins jump from satellite images, as Dr. Billy had inferred.

Judy had said I'd have been lesser without my supplements. But I wasn't so sure, especially now. What I really wondered was if something more was at my core, at anyone's core, beyond chemicals and maintenance. Identity isn't static, so who am I at any one point in time? Who is anyone? Just a snapshot. A demarcation of place in relation to. A point on an X/Y axis. I am what I am, I thought.

If X then Y. If Hannah over time, with V., she becomes:

    A) *someone else*

    B) *herself*

    C) *a chimera of I's*

    D) *a multiplicity of indeterminacy.*

XXIX.

I was in the nurse's hands next. I described my mental lapses. Gray outs. Brain scores falling. The treatments I'd had after Tigue. Increased doses. Forever the inability to feel. Regarding my treatment, the nurse said it was impossible to isolate a memory before it spreads.

"But how long does it take to rebuild a foundation?"

"It depends. It seems you should've recovered by now."

What am I supposed to do with this? I thought.

"What are we supposed to do with this?" I asked.

"First thing is lay off V."

"Okay, yes, I'd like that. But how do I tell Judy?"

"Judy?"

"Her mother, head of the Learning Committee," Azzie offered.

"Ah, yes, I see—"

"Wait, there are good uses for V.?" Azzie asked. "I mean..."

The nurse hesitated. "You could argue for some. You know the reasons why you're taking. Inevitably, though, your mental shape changes. You become dependent. I could show you some cross sections of activated brains."

"No, really, that's ok." Azzie scowled.

"There are plenty of studies."

"Huh?"

"As you know, Lumena is a hub for research. They've funded many studies whose results aren't in their best interest to release."

"How do you have access?"

She ignored my question. "I'm sure you've seen the lines of people my age, you know, chronic over-accumulators who keep paying in. It's too late."

"To stop?"

"Sure."

"No one talks about long-term effects," I said. I told her how I'd seen my father just blankety-blank as he wandered, no words, seemingly locked inside of himself. "That's typical of early decline," the nurse said. She had this sympathetic look which made me know it was bad.

I knew Harold's mind wasn't sharp in so many ways but this confirmed it was slipping.

"But what can I do?" I asked.

"There are no easy answers. Ask questions. Hold the factory accountable."

"I'm always shut down."

"Then continue. How much longer until you finish school?"

"Three semesters."

"Well, hold off but start in earnest then."

"But how can I not now?"

"I mean, I don't know what to say. You shouldn't even be here. Do what you can to get by in the meantime."

The nurse took Celia for a blood draw and to run more tests. Azzie and I walked back down the hill and we sat beside the pomegranate trees, which resembled overgrown shrubs. It felt so odd to sit there doing nothing with nothing to scroll through. My mind reeled with thoughts of my father Harold, his mental gaps, and there was nothing I could do about it.

Azzie turned to me, "You know, up at the house when you were asleep, they were talking about the fire." She said she'd been resting on a very plush couch in an anteroom waiting for Jules to return with word on my state, and she'd just taken a handful of AnxietEZ because she was so worked up about this and about me, and in this brief moment of utter relaxation a squabble in the next room had spilled over and intruded on her peace. I asked her who had squabbled, and she said wasn't sure. I asked if anything lurid had been said, and she shrugged and said it was nothing we hadn't already heard.

One person said something about the factory fire and toxicities being "very fucked up" and the other person started talking rapidly in a way she had trouble following about the heaves, and toxicities, the water not being safe to drink. The other person had responded, "To each action, an equal and opposite reaction."

"OK, and what does that mean?"

"I'm just telling you. I have my suspicions."

"That they're concerned about the seepage?"

Azzie said, "Yeah but, I don't know..." She took a pomegranate that had fallen, held it cupped in her palm. "Maybe it was like this! Like they rolled a grenade in? Or did they deliver an explosive? Concealed it and then—" She threw it to the ground, the fruit cracked open and rolled.

It was anticlimactic. I was appalled by the red seeds tumbling.

"Probably neither?" It seemed entirely possible, plausible, really, that they wanted to thwart the fucked-upness of system, but that didn't mean they'd set the fire. It didn't seem to be either/or. *Either/Or*, as I knew from class, was the first text by Kierkegaard, the old school philosopher who saw the choice of human action as being either one way or another. A dichotomy rather than a continuum. I realized I'd only seen one way of being but had spent my life dreaming about what that other way might look like. And here we were, between.

If these women had been involved, it would almost be heroic. But that didn't offset the disaster that had been unleashed. Or the panic. That was two days ago already.

I wondered about the other missing pieces. Most of it, I was sure, I couldn't guess, much like the dark matter that makes up 95% of the universe. Who can fathom the extent of the material we can't see that holds our world in place—like these resistors who had been out here living parallel in time. I'd been oblivious.

All is as it had never seemed, I realized—all of those mornings where I'd lay in bed groggy with a faint sense of myself, pre-dosing, before taking my V. At those moments my body felt almost like I inhabited it, not like the usual split, if that's what you'd call it, of material and immaterial, vegetal, mineral, aspirational. I knew so few pleasures, but as I'd lay there half awake, my tablet rousing me from sleep, vibrating against my body. I was inspired with feeling—like ice cream on a summer day, like a hot shower fogging the mirror in the morning. All this before VALEDICTORIAN's numbness set in again—as if I'd never felt a thing.

Azzie and I went back to the mulch piles where we had a view of the house. We climbed to the top of the largest pile, and we each leaned back into its softness. Azzie took a tab from her case. Offered me one. I took it, swallowed it. I didn't even ask what it was. I started to feel light and smooth inside for the first time in a while. Azzie pushed herself up against me and told me I had the cutest belly. She started tracing my belly button with her finger, then buzzing her lips against it in a way that tickled. I pushed her off and told her to stop messing. I asked her if her feet were as sore as mine.

"The worst," she said, and shoved a foot in my face.

"You are so disgusting," I said lovingly as I rolled over on her and pinned her with all my weight. She was so intimately disgusting, and I loved her and she repulsed me.

I thought it was so odd how we're all marked by this former tether to our mothers. Judy liked to say I'd been born without a cord. She always said it with such awe. Harold had confirmed this wasn't true, that they feared the cord was decaying and so they'd gone into surgery. Judy said I'd just appeared from behind a series of scrubs and screens. I was a green-eyed monster and had a full head of hair. I'm pretty sure she'd used the word monster, though I knew she meant this affectionately. She'd said she'd been sorry to miss the whole vaginal birth experience, as she put it, but knowing her she was more grateful that her vag was left intact. She'd told me of how she was given an IV line of supplements to promote bonding and love through presence and touch—or possibly instead of—and how she'd never anticipated such a rush. She talked of how her milk hadn't even descended. It was

the way she and I had always been.
   You are the luckiest, she'd say.
   And I'd answer, *To be born into this?*
   She never had a response that made sense.
   Blame my cats, or something.

"The liberated mind was born violently, an act of planetary suicide."

XXX. STEADY STATE MAINTENANCE

Harold sat at his desk as video monitors tracked trajectories of satellites whirling about. He'd been sitting in the same space every day for so long the carpet was worn under the wheels of his chair. As he sat there, he started to wonder about this heaviness. Empathy wasn't making any of this easier.

He used to be able to judge the work ahead by the piles of papers before him. He had spent days pushing papers to other desks and shredding documents. But now the desk was empty except for his two screens. He reviewed funding for on-the-ground and in-the-air technologies. Equipment for exploration was a priority: satellites, rocket launchers, space stations, investigational equipment. But it was all immaterial, so close to imagined that he'd forget the work awaited him in an endless queue.

This wasn't what he'd imagined for his fifth decade. What had he thought when he was Hannah's age? He'd don a space suit. Take off. Throttle. Colonize distant planets? *Anything was possible.* The idea was now laughable. No one had told him that time is a funnel you fall through.

Words were coming so much better with Empathy. He knew now where they waited. But all of this silence. There were so many vacant spaces and all of this feeling. Where was Judy night after night as he sat at home? And Hannah. He hadn't seen her since before the fire. And she hadn't even bothered to check in. Had her friend send a text to tell him she was staying over. He stared out the window looking at people like ants on the ground below, setting up concrete blocks and latticework. In the distance, he saw the south side of Factory Hill, the stacks of scaffolds and steel beams, and a Caterpillar pushing mounds. He used to love looking at the factory with its smoke rising, the trucks mounting the hill. So much happened there, with so many chemicals forming, transforming, making their way toward bodies in need. He shook just thinking of the current devastation.

With so much done it seemed there was still just as much to do. For his expedience in thinking over so many years, what did he have to show for it? A series of timestamps that he could scroll through. Bank statements available for download. The end of one day lay beside another, shifting to weeks and years. He'd spent at least two hundred days at this desk each year, if not more; in thirty years then, what did that amount to? 7,000 days, 72,000 hours—is this what life was measured by?

How was this not Hannah's future too? Except she was resistant to school, to the possibilities of what she could do. He didn't blame her, though he worried.

Her fruit-mind was morphing and her scores were falling. He wished he could talk to her. Maybe next time he saw her? Question was, where had she gone off to and when would she return?

So busy, Judy messaged, interrupting his mental drift. *You wouldn't believe the pressure. This is really eating at me Har.*

DM from Judy, again. This time her face image appeared on the device—eye bags, hair back, bleary-eyes apparent.

Why didn't he do something? What would he say—that it's going to be okay? He was so cloudy-headed. He messaged her back to say yes, he'd come to her talk that evening. He assured her it would work out. Harold looked up and his colleague Greg was standing there in the doorway. Greg, the quality slacks and tie guy. Something in the way he looked and then sat in the swivel chair made Harold appreciative. Harold nodded.

Greg said he'd seen Judy on the news.

Harold shrugged. *No hope*, he thought.

Greg asked how Hannah was doing.

Harold started to cry.

"Oh man, I didn't mean to make you..." He looked embarrassed. "This has been hard on everyone."

Harold appreciated Greg's attempts to console him. He said, "No, no, it's fine," when really it wasn't, when really his next thought was of Hannah and her absence. He thought, *What do I even really know about my daughter?* He tried to think of all the things: she hated peas, late at night she'd get up for a glass of grapefruit soda, light poured from under her door at all hours, she resented Judy's insistence on anything. She liked to gaze out from their roof deck; he liked her thin tapered fingers; she had her mother's tenacity and his tendency to mental drift, unfortunately. Greenish-brown eyes like the deep sea; took V. erratically, had animal companions; when she was younger she'd made him feel needed.

He felt so embarrassed at how short his list was. The more he wanted to stop the tears, the faster they came. "I don't know where to begin…"

Greg got up, left the room, and returned with a box of tissues. Said he wanted to help. Was there anything he could do?

Harold nodded between heaves and tried to say *thank you* but it all got mangled with his weird breathing. He took a deep breath, set his monitors to sleep, and pushed away the quiver in his chest. He managed to say, "Not sure what you can do. Will ask Judy, but of course, I'm very busy."

Greg nodded. "Yes, of course," and took this cue to leave.

Harold turned on his screen and his futile attempt to track Hannah's location. No pings. He realized he needed new ways to handle his sensitivity.

[MAKING THE MOST OF YOUR EMPATHY] brought to you by
ASTRALROX

Like emerging from a fog. Navigating your new emotions can
be thrilling and curious, but also overwhelming at times. With
strengthened neural pathways, there's so much newfound joy
to experience. You may not know exactly how to handle this at
first.

We have developed exercises to make sure you make the most
of your new empathy and connectivity, to introduce the joy and
excitement of living and (re)connecting to the everyday.

1. ATTENTION: Is there a relationship that you've neglected?
    Now that you've emerged from the fog do you feel distant?
    Envision this person. In what way do you want to relate?

2. LISTEN: Begin a correspondence. Start a conversation with
    someone unfamiliar. You may be sitting next to him on the
    bus, waiting in line at lunch. Look for something interest-
    ing. Contact one of the people on your list, tell them that
    you'd like to be in better touch.

3. VALIDATE: another's opinion. Engage. Respond with words
    that identify you listened and that you care. Recognize the
    emotions emanating from their skin, their lips, in the scent
    of their breath. Ask them questions in response to this.
    Make a mental list. Acknowledge their existence.

XXXI. PHARMACOVIGILANCE

Judy was surprised to see the auditorium filled with bodies and lined with balloons bearing the LUMENA logo. She didn't want this ill-suited detail to distract her. She wanted to stand assured before the sea of bodies multiplying as they filled aisles. She was surprised to see Harold shuffle in and take a seat in the back row. This brought her calm; he could be of use. Billy was seated in the front with her. She would attempt to mimic his assurance.

He introduced her warmly—perhaps less warmly than she'd prefer, though more warmly than was welcome here. Not as warm as a shared bed but definitely warmer than a cold, hard desk. Billy said her perseverance had helped tremendously. She knew she'd helped him in other ways too.

Stone faces stared. There was a hush as she took the podium.

"How do you remain calm during an emergency? What's the secret? I've been asked this repeatedly in the last twenty-four hours and my answer is two things: fluidity and focus. Picture a glass of water shattering. Assess the situation. How do you direct its flow and absorb the spill? Sweep up the shards if nothing else. Do you worry? Panic? These don't do a thing to assist. Remember. Keep your wits about you."

"But what if our needs aren't being met!?" a voice yelled out.

"Simplify. Don't become blocked by your anger or frustration. Look for the most direct route. If this means acquiring V., consider your options: what supply remains, that's the availability, consider allocations and stockpiles."

"We don't have time!" This voice sounded blustery and short of breath.

A hush.

Judy couldn't see faces. The stage lights were too bright. She didn't know how her message was being received. She sensed it wasn't. She felt wearied knees and chest heave. Her assuredness wasn't calming the crowd.

"Some of these kids are acting like zombies."

"Rumors, these are simply rumors," Judy repeated.

"Nah, it's true!" A woman stood up and denounced, "They're not right. I've seen it in my kids, the neighbors' kids, all around. They just stare, act like no one's there."

Breathe, Judy thought. "Just breathe," Judy said.

"What's she saying?"

"Don't panic."

"Is she talking to herself?!" The murmur below her voice rose.

She thought, *don't panic*. "Listen!" she responded

with all the force she could muster. "Grogginess is a sign of V.'s abrupt discontinuation. It rarely happens with tapering. This will get better. Give it a day or two."

"How do we know that's true?"

"I have literature." She nodded to Billy and he pointed to a QR code projected onto the wall. She felt like she was at the stake, or that she would be soon. Her words were slipping past them. "We'll pull through. We will begin releasing allocations. We should all focus on what we can do."

"I'll tell you. Our kids are not lab rats!"

"We're working on it. It takes time to increase production. We are assessing the methods and logistics."

The crowd became a sea and the sea a wave and they were no longer in their seats but instead flowing toward the stage. Angry faces before her seemed to magnify so she could only see glaring eyes. Then there were just the empty hands before her, palms open, reaching for her, hands, shoulders, coat and hem. *Doesn't being here count for something?* She reached for her 4 Steps Plus 4, pushed the papers into those hands. Paper gave them something to hold on to but mostly the sheets slipped to the floor. Hands empty again, mouths turning to scowls.

She took a deep breath. She eyed Billy. He had his back to her. He was hunched over and whispering into Maxine's ear.

"Anger can be a tremendous catalyst," she said.

"Release the supplies, it's our children's minds!"

"In due time."

They gathered around her, all huff and screech.

"I have a daughter, too," is all she could eke out.

"And where is she? Probably sitting on a pile of V."

"We're all taking a hit."

"Right, I see it now, she's got a stockpile."

"A river of V. and she's swimming in it."

Judy wondered if they knew about the box in her bag? She felt like they did, like they might attack her just to see if it existed. Judy's instincts were telling her to leave swiftly, but she couldn't exactly make a beeline.

"It's not that way at all," she insisted.

"But isn't it?"

Palms turned to fists as if about to swing and then the tide turned and the women receded, somehow, miraculously. Their feet moved toward the doors.

Judy looked out the second-floor window. The block below was cordoned off. Lights hit the walls in rhythmic blue-then-white. Women held hands as they walked down the street, arm-in-arm the bodies connected and the space they took grew. The spaces between them contracted as they stood shoulder to shoulder, flanked by shields on either side.

XXXII. INDUCTION OF ALTERNATE STATES

I began to wonder if they'd forgotten about us down here. Daylight was disappearing but I could see light up on the hill, like someone was lighting a line of torches. I couldn't remember the last time that I'd eaten but I felt nauseous more than anything. Two people carrying lanterns were moving down the hill toward us. I soon recognized Celia running with a woman following behind her. The woman took steps in a calculated way as if to counter Celia's pace.

Celia was quick to make introductions. "Here they are—see? HannahAzu, this is Jai."

Jai didn't smile. I wasn't sure if the muscles in her face could align to make this happen. Jai wasn't who I'd expected, though I'm not sure who I'd expected other than someone else. She towered over us, wide-shouldered and strong. She looked like she'd be able to carry two patients at once.

Jai nodded to acknowledge us but looked preoccupied. Her eyes were sunken as if she'd used charcoal to line her lids. It was impressive, this. The inked lines on her hands, they looked almost cryptic, extending up her sleeves. Jai responded as if no time had passed in this long pause.

She looked to Celia, "Not everyone would do this

for a friend." Then she turned to us, "You risked plenty to come but still, you shouldn't be here. We can't welcome you in the ways we would if circumstances were different."

We shrugged. Okay, yes, whatever that meant. The way she said this sounded stiff.

"We insisted," Azzie jumped in, "on coming. We were only going to come so far but then Hannah and her condition..."

Curiosity kills the cat. It's like Jai thought this the way she stared at me.

"I've heard. You must not mention this to anyone."

"If it's about keeping secrets, I can keep a secret," I said.

Azzie agreed that she was a secret-keeper too. I didn't say anything contrary to this though I knew she wasn't the best at it.

Jai seemed to consider this and said, "Okay, good." I could tell she didn't say what she was thinking. "We can give you shelter for the night. But you need to leave first thing tomorrow."

I said that I had questions first.

Jai nodded.

"We want to know why you made Celia come out here. I mean, given her condition. Like, aren't there things she could've done at home? I mean, less drastic?"

"Do you know what would've happened if she had

stayed on the ward?"

"Not really."

"It's not good."

"Obviously."

"Look. Your question is valid—but I don't have answers. At least not anything I can get into."

"That's all you have to say?"

"Perhaps it will make more sense soon. But until then, I'd say trust your gut."

"Well, I feel like retching."

"Then trust the reasons you helped her."

This didn't address my questions but it made me curious. In Lumena, no one says, *Trust what you feel.* They say, *Trust us. Take this.*

Jai said she was glad for the introduction, but that she had to get back up to the house, and that we should wait here until Marj came to get us. There would be a dinner. They were expecting friends. For now, she said, we shouldn't talk to anyone we hadn't already met.

Jai left her lantern with us, and Celia climbed up and sat beside us in near darkness. My assessment was Jai seemed gruff but fair. In the dim light Celia looked relieved but also exhausted. I supposed we all were.

"So that's Jai, huh?"

Celia nodded. "See, she's not scary. I told you she's been very busy."

"She didn't seem enamored with us."

"You aren't even supposed to be here, boos."

"So what happened up there," I asked, "after we left?"

Celia shrugged, "Nothing really, the nurse talked to Marj, I think, and then consulted with the others about whether I'm well enough to leave in the morning. I guess it's not too serious because I'm cleared to go."

"Is that what you want?" I asked.

"Of course it is."

I didn't respond. I couldn't help but question what was for the best. I was relieved we'd made it here and that Jai had arrived. She seemed determined to help Celia but I just hoped her help wasn't some fucked idea of assistance. It was hard to say with everyone being so closed-mouthed about what was really happening.

Azzie had been abnormally quiet through this. "You doing okay?" I asked her.

She nodded, moved closer to Celia, placed her arms around her and pulled her close, "I just can't imagine going back without you."

I couldn't either.

"Don't be silly, goose," Celia nuzzled her, placing her cheek against Azzie's neck. "I heart you two. I will see you again and again."

I wasn't so sure of this. I could tell this didn't sway

Azzie either. For the first time I realized there was a possibility we really wouldn't see Celia again—and that people made the choice to stay out here. I wondered if that's what Azzie was thinking about too.

Marj finally came down to us holding two lanterns and apologized for making us wait. She handed one lantern to Azzie and directed us to a line of square-faced grills that had been set up by the shelter. It wasn't far from the wolf dog's chain, which was now hanging loose. Marj doused the coals with a fluid, then lit a match, and threw it in. She asked if we knew how to tend a fire.

I laughed.

She said, never mind, that she would do that, and she'd bring out the foods. We'd just have to turn them every so often. We'd need to watch closely and remove them from the grill before they burned.

This we could do. Or at least attempt to.

She told us to refrain from conversations with the guests. We were her nieces if it came up.

"But what names should we use?" Celia asked.

Marj said that anyone here should know not to ask. She told us she had to go feed the dog and tend to a few things but that she'd come back shortly and when she did we could fix ourselves plates of food.

Guests started to arrive. Azzie said she'd seen a few up at the house. They arrived bearing bags of vegetables, loaves of bread, fish, animal limbs. One woman carried a pan with a boar's head, its snout sticking up. She set it on a table near us and Azzie started poking at its skin, then held the pan up in front of her face as if it were a mask.

"Stop!" I demanded, "It's ghastly!"

"And I'm a ghoul," Azzie laughed.

Marj came back and asked us to place it on the grill Celia looked disgusted.

"I'll stick to the veg," I said.

Azzie stepped in to assist. Marj explained that they tried to use all parts of the animals they slaughter This was a wild boar. I knew it was an invasive species here, without predators. The hog head smelled sweetly of roasted meat. The scent made me feel ravenous, but not the thought of eating its eyes, ears, and cheeks.

I heard the wolf dog howling in the distance.

Marj took some meat and veggie skewers from the grill, then loaded it with more. She said Celia needed to go with her. There was a meal for her up at the house. Azzie and I were to stay and keep an eye on the grills but we could eat whatever we liked from the food they'd set out.

We filled our plates and sat on the ground. I could hear wisps of conversations but not enough to make sense of any one thread.

"You know, they don't look like what I'd envisioned—the people out here," I told Azzie. "I mean, I realize I'd never imagined them with faces. Isn't that bizarre?"

Azzie didn't seem to think so.

I had also thought they'd be seductive, secretive, and intriguing. Dark haired. With red cravats. Faces in shadows. Types I'd seen in movies. I knew too that Shelley had written a poem in support of anarchy, declaring the need for individual freedom and to fight against thugs in power. This was after he'd gotten kicked out of school. He was in favor of overthrowing rulers for a system of self-government. These women were of the same mind in some ways. But also, these women wouldn't stand out within town limits. They wore long sleeves and hiking boots, and though they looked less kempt than the average person I figured that had to do with circumstances, like proximity to showers.

Azzie was concentrating on the beans and meats she'd piled on her plate. I asked what she was thinking. She looked up and said she was thinking about reasons why someone would stay.

"Would you want to?"

"No. Not now, not ever. I'd be itchy and sweaty and bored forever. And besides, I'd run out of these." She pulled out her pill case.

I said, "I mean, it could be intriguing. There have to be all kinds of people—abandoned lovers, bands of outsiders. Could be an adventure. It might not be as bad as you think."

Seeing the women gathered here made me realize it could be done and that it was being done. They'd been kind of weird and cagey, but also, they'd been kind enough given the circumstances.

Azzie looked offended. "Hannah. You've lost it."

"I'm no convert."

"You say that." She opened her pill case, tapped a yellow triangle, a green circle, and a red ball into her palm, then swallowed.

I wondered if she worried she'd lose me too.

"Well, I'll leave all the fleas and lice and vermin for you," I said to her sweetly.

"You're the animal lover. I would miss bathing too."

"Marj does have a certain scent about her."

Azzie laughed. I felt good being able to make her do that.

When Marj returned she asked Azzie and me to help prepare the after-dinner drinks. She led us down a ravine to the fire pit where a flame had already been lit. She took us to a cabin and led us into a room with cupboards filled with teas and bulk ingredients. Marj took out many mugs, placed them on trays. And then she took a large strainer into which she spooned different herbs and dried plants. She asked us to help carry all of this to the fire, and said that the rest of the group would move down here soon.

There she prepared the tea over a tremendous pot.

As the others migrated down the hill to the fire, we handed out mugs. Eventually Marj handed mugs to both of us.

"A fortifier," she said.

The tea was smooth like honey but tasted like vinegar.

Marj said we could join them for the end of the evening. We sat on stumps laid by the outer edge of the fire.

They were talking of animal auras and energy fields. Jai said she was a jaguar. But the woman who'd brought the boar's head objected. She said no, Jai was more like a stubborn mare.

Jai protested: "I'm not soft or motherly!"

"Mares are strong. A force to contend with. You're more of one than you'd like to admit."

They laughed. They spoke of the ash in Lumena, the toxicities from the fire spreading, and its potential to kill more plant and animal life within a many-mile radius. Apparently, there were more fires to the west, and further off, there were factory-run sites set up to mine more minerals used for supplements and to build more intricate motherboards.

We'd taken minerals, displaced animals, destroyed forests without any thought, and to harness what—

Nature's soul was slipping away, they said. I didn't buy into this idea of soul and sacred, though I'd never heard it used in quite this way. It had always been apparent to me from a very young age that the words *soul* and *sacred* were symbolic, more a reflection of a desire to find meaning than anything else. But as they said this, I realized I felt disconnected. I didn't possess an essence, or if I did, I didn't know what it was.

Jai moved her hands for emphasis as she spoke, and her hands grew larger and began to emit trails of light.

I thought I saw chimps in the distance, riding in four wheelers over the paths. Two came much closer with teas in hand, their mouths agape, heads back and big teeth shining. They were laughing, at what?

I closed my eyes, thinking they might disappear.

I opened them. The chimps were now nestled in the trees. There were lights shining brilliantly behind and above them in the night sky.

"Do you see?" I whispered to Azzie.

"See what?"

"The colors moving across the sky. I think it must be aurora borealis."

The women now had a halo around them, as if the fire had engulfed them. Jules had returned and was among them. "There used to be so many kinds of acorns," she said. "And just as many words to describe the trees they fall from: *Holly, holm, Quercus ilex*."

"Can you name ten?" someone looked toward us and asked.

We just sat there.

"How about five?"

"Trees?" I shook my head.

"My point exactly. Landscape generates language, shapes our idea of what our world is made of."

I didn't appreciate being used to make her point. But I did wonder what words would describe me and my life: *Fruit, rot, fall?*

"Kids today can't tell a porpoise from a manatee."

This wasn't true but I didn't say so. I imagined I'd know the difference if I encountered either in person. I thought of the endangered species list and how I'd never encountered any of those animals IRL, in nature, or whatever, but somehow I still felt their absence. It wasn't something I could point to but rather a concavity.

Soon I saw a chimp ambling, then two, then more, moving in to form a circle beyond ours. No one seemed to notice as they inched forward, closer, now pointing and laughing.

"What!? What's so funny?" I asked.

The women stopped talking and turned abruptly, looking out into the darkness then back at me.

Some laughed with the chimps and others looked uneasy.

Jules came and sat next to me. She patted my back. "It's okay honey."

"Here they are all playful and laughing."

"—maybe you need to lie down?"

I shrugged her off. "I'm fine." I closed my eyes for a second and by the time I opened them the chimps had vanished.

Marj was talking about time, how it was a cone and our lives were unspooling alongside so many past lives, and conjuring the ancient spirits of inhabitants and beasts, woolly mammoths, shamans performing ceremonies for rain and fertility, humping the ground and ejaculating; harnessing nature's energy. Before that even. Molten rock. We needed to remain aware of the land's dimensions.

As night grew later, we formed a cluster, and I grew more aware of myself expanding as I stood next to Azzie and we looked up at the stars like a comet had splintered.

The women continued to talk and their words and phrases became opaque. Like I was listening to a score. It all ran together. All that was left was awareness of my body expanding to fill the atmosphere.

I could only see what was immediately before me. One chimp was busy taking stones from the ground and throwing them into the fire. Another came over and placed her arm around me and held her cup of tea to my mouth, then dropped it suddenly. She started pounding her chest. I started imitating her, pounding my chest too. Other chimps dropped what they were doing and now a dozen of us stood before the fire. Some were gnawing on bamboo and then holding the ends to the flame. I grabbed a shoot, placed it in the fire, let it cool. I noticed some chimps lying on the ground.

So many side by side. It looked like their scars made a pattern—lines interconnected into a series of verticals and diagonals interspersed with punctuation relating to points of light.

I wanted to step back, take it all in. I felt like if I stared at it long enough, I'd be able to comprehend.

Some women came over. They too held shoots over the fire. I got down on my hands and knees so I could get a closer look at the chimps. When I was down on the ground, a chimp held the bamboo to the fire then touched down on my skin. Pain shot through me, electrifying. The pain faded quickly into relief. Wave after wave washed over.

I looked up and saw Jai's face. She was angry. She pulled me up by the arm and said, "What the hell, Hannah?"

The chimps suddenly took leave. I looked around and saw just the women from dinner surrounding me, their mouths coiled like figure eights, their eyes falling into their faces.

I laughed awkwardly. It was terrible.

The women gathered around as if they might now devour me. Jai just stared at me with fire in her face.

Jules broke in and pulled me under her arm. "Let me take you to bed."

I went with her and pleaded to not leave me alone, that Jai was rabid. She shushed me and said I'd just had too much tea. She needed me to be quiet and she'd lead me to the bed that had been made for me. Azzie was there, already asleep.

XXXIII.

By the time I woke I was sweaty and the sunlight was bright through the window. Azzie was up—and had been for a while. She said she'd been knocked flat by the tea.

"What was in it?" she asked me.

"No clue."

Azzie was not the type to nap in uncomfortable places, but she'd fallen asleep by the fire. She'd been woken up and led here to the cabin. She didn't recall by whom. So many gaps in her memory.

"—there was a ritual," I said, "like some kind of ceremony? There was this script written across their backs."

"Let me guess—"

"I know it sounds sus, but I swear there were chimps."

"Hannah." She looked perplexed but tired mostly.

"Maybe their spirits?"

"Do you think Jai and all were as gone as we were?"

"Probably? I know you don't believe me but look." I lifted my shirt and showed her my back.

"What happened!?"

"Hurts like fuck. The chimps had bamboo they were burning over the fire and...."

"Stop it with the chimps. But that wound's raw. You need to clean it."

"And then Jai started raging at me."

"Jai's angry? None of this makes sense. Maybe we should see if they're up? I mean they'd said they're leaving."

"...and Celia's going too."

"I know."

We washed our faces in a stream that ran just behind the cabin, and then walked up to the house to see if we could find anyone. The wolf dog ran toward us until the chain yanked him back. He ran back and forth, marking a quarter circle in the dirt as he growled.

Azzie growled back. We were not morning persons.

We went inside the trailer to look for Marj but she was gone. The house was empty too.

"They wouldn't have left the dog," Azzie said.

"Let's sit and wait. Someone has to come back this way."

And so we sat like doddering old men looking at their lawns waiting for them to grow. Eventually I spotted Jules in the distance, walking toward us. I felt like I'd never been so happy to see someone.

"I was at the cabin just now," she said. "I was worried you'd left."

I laughed. That was absurd. "We thought the same about you."

"How's your back?" Jules asked.

"It hurts."

"It looks terrible. What happened?" Azzie demanded.

"—Marj shouldn't have given you that tea."

"What was in it?"

"Mushrooms, clarifying. Wormwood, or a derivative? I don't think she knew it would have such a strong effect."

More drugs. More augmentation. More chemicals. Actually natural, yes, but how was this different from Lumena? I knew Jules was possibly lying to us but she didn't have reason to, I didn't think.

"Come with me. I'll take you to say your goodbyes and then we'll go over how you'll get home."

We walked with Jules past the cabins and fire pit and followed a trail into the woods. A red Jeep was parked just off the path with a trailer attached behind it. Jai was loading the trailer. Celia sat across the backseat of the Jeep. Something about her face looked refreshed.

"So you're doing this?" I asked.

"You know you don't have to," Azzie coaxed.

"That's ridiculous. Why would I come all this way and not want to?"

"You can change your mind is all."

"Oh birdies, boo."

"I mean, there are other ways to get by in Lumena."

"You know they'd put me right back on the ward. I'd never get out with my mind intact."

"Truth," I said. It was. "But also—there's a lot we don't know about them."

"I know enough. More than you'd think. Does it matter, though? Loves, I'm free."

"And?"

"I'm not looking back. I love you two. Thank you for this. It's the best gift. Bises, both of you."

"I still don't feel good about this."

"Do you know they drugged us last night?" Azzie said.

Celia shook her head. Her brow furrowed a bit.

"The tea..."

"Maybe they're concerned about what you remember?"

"I mean, that's *so* sus..."

"I don't trust them," Azzie added. "I mean, how can we trust they'll take care of you?"

Jai came over. She had a bandana tied across her brow. She said they were leaving soon and that she was sorry. She wanted to talk to Azzie and me alone.

"Celia can hear whatever you have to say," Azzie said.

Jai agreed to this. "Look. I'm sorry I lost it when you fell into the fire last night. We can't risk anything happening to you two."

"I remember it differently—"

"I'm sure you do. I didn't know you'd been given the tea. I thought you were being careless. I wasn't in the right mind to deal, either, honestly."

"We didn't know what was in the tea," I said.

"I know. I don't think Marj realized... I mean, I would've stopped her. But there are so many moving parts with this early departure."

"Well, ok whatever," I said.

Jai told us no, that we deserved an apology, and that we'd done the right thing, bringing Celia here. She said our hearts were in the right place.

She turned to me, placed her hand on my shoulder—"Your side," she said, "it will heal quickly." She said Jules would give me a salve to keep it from scaring. Jules would also put us in touch with a contact in Lumena. Then she went back to packing the jeep.

"But how do we get in touch? How will we know you're okay?" I asked Celia.

Celia said she'd write to us.

Jai added, "But not for a while."

Communications would be minimal if at all, at first, but eventually they'd reach us. Messages would be sent and we would recognize them when they arrived.

I wanted to think, *well yes, of course this is good, isn't it?*

But I didn't feel it.

We were abandoning her, and I envied her.

Jules took us back to the house, where Azzie and I grabbed our sacks and water bottles. She said she'd help us prepare for the hike back. She would give us a ride back to the stream, and from there we'd follow it back to the field. We'd walk away, with our backs to the stream and would know we were going the right direction if the sun stayed behind us. We'd be back before we knew it, she said. It was the first time I realized we'd really have to return to our own snafu of a situation.

She couldn't give us a map or any material directions. She wrote down some names of landmarks we might see—blind man's hill, eagle's perch, a waterfall, a place called devil's tub. I didn't think this would help. She said it didn't matter, that she'd set us on the right path. She also gave us a handwritten list of edible plants with hand drawn illustrations. "I don't think you'll need this now, but maybe at some point?"

She gave us packs of dried fruits and nuts and mushrooms, a filter to make the river water drinkable, and advised us it was best not to use the filter until the toxicities cleared, but we could in an emergency. She gave us capsules filled with lavender colored powder. Said it was an herbal remedy for detox, stabilization of minds in transition. She also handed me a glass jar filled with something gelatinous. It was an emollient for my back. She said I should keep the burn covered. No bathing suits, no open backs. Not until it healed. If anyone asked, I'd taken a tumble. Too much Delixir. No word about being out here. I nodded. No trouble, I intended no trouble, I said, especially for Celia.

Jules estimated that we would arrive by midafternoon if we walked at a steady pace. She gave us a name and address for a friend we should get in touch with once we were back, but to wait for a bit, until the soot and all had settled.

We climbed into one of those four-wheelers I'd seen the day before and she drove us over small winding paths, down ravines, and over rocky shoals. Jules parked by the stream, gave us each a hug, and said, "Take care of yourselves."

She nodded when I looked back, as if to ask if we were really going the right way?

Once we'd made a distance, I heard her yell: "See you again soon—you hear?"

Along the way Azzie and I made a game. We called it friend or foe. The premise was one person would point to an animal or a rock or a plant or a structure and identify it as one or the other. The person who didn't point would either punch or hug. We didn't say much to each other about returning.

Between us: the sound of leaves crushing under feet.

WHAT TO EAT
morel shiitake truffle (protein)
kudzu, heliotropic green
dandelion blossom, edible weeds
wild elderberry and wild blackberry
ponderosa pine, maple sap—lick from tree
honeysuckle amaranth
cattails/punks/bullrush
rhizomes, boil and eat

WHAT TO AVOID
milky sap,
thorny briar patch,
trifecta of leaves
almond scent
cyanide dream
beans bulbs seeds

XXXIV.

Jules had given us each a sandwich made from left-overs from the night before. I ate mine quickly and still felt famished. The longer we walked the less we talked and the more I realized that Azzie was preoccupied. I guess I was too. She wasn't plying me with her usual chatter. She looked pale and sweaty. I asked if she was feeling okay.

She said she was just sad, "Like, if anything happens to Celia..."

"Don't I know it ..."

"Do you?"

"Sure"

"But I love her."

"I love her, too."

"Not the same."

"Why?"

"I feel like I'm her protector."

"Bringing her out here, you were just trying to help her."

"Which makes it worse." She seemed more upset than me, suddenly. I can't explain why but I felt liberated knowing this. The more I thought about it the more I thought about the fluidity between the three of us, the potential energy, our love, and how it flowed between us.

I stayed a few steps behind for a while and gave Azzie some space. I felt sad too, knowing that nothing had changed really. We were heading home. I had no instincts, and if I were alone I would definitely die out here.

I appreciated Azzie so simply. A body in this with me. The ways she was my sister and the way she nuzzled my neck, the way she was so free and I was so often not, and the way we rolled up our pants and took off our shoes and ran into the stream. Cold water washed over our legs. Tiny tadpoles slipped through our hands. Our mouths became whispers, we traced our toes through silt and sand.

My back was sore, my feet were caked in dirt and my face was cracking in the sun but the ground was holding me.

No more words between us as we walked, just comrades exchanging glances, fingers pointing, swatting flies, shielding our eyes from the sun's glare. Yellow flowers blossoming in tall grass, a patch of wild blackberries. Out here was another thing altogether.

Soon we saw smokestacks far above the trees, still standing in the distance, as if they were marking the burned-out crater of Factory Hill. It looked as if steel beams had sprouted from the ground, and tall metal cranes dotted the landscape. A new building was taking shape as we stood there, it seemed.

Azzie grabbed me. "Stop!"

"What?"

"We can't cross back. Not yet."

"We're doing this one way or another."

"I mean yes, okay, but I'm still not okay with leaving her out there. I mean, here. I mean in the forest, with them."

"But we already left her."

"Leaving the woods is leaving her for real. We can't come back. And we can't tell anyone."

I hadn't anticipated this part. It was like we'd just helped Celia tube over a waterfall and we weren't sticking around to see if she made the descent intact.

"And we have to get our story straight," she insisted.

I chewed on the nuts and fruits Jules had given us while we talked about what we'd say, which, fundamentally was nothing, nada. I'd say I had blacked out, Azzie had found me, and we went back to her place to shelter together, and we were so preoccupied with the effects of the fire that we kept streaming the news about the factory, slept odd hours, or not at all. That time passed. We wouldn't mention Celia or Jai or crossing boundaries. We agreed on that, but I sensed we had different reasons for it.

I looked to the smokestacks, and I envisioned that soon enough the new structure would be standing and these stacks again would be emitting clouds and

290

casting a tinge of sweetness over the town, while networks of computers and microchips processed, while conveyor belts shuttled powders and pills, while making the multitudinous chemicals that made us feel one way or another or not at all.

I was born into this dependence but now I knew I could break from it too.

How does grass grow from seed? Leaves bend toward the sun, generate photosynthetic energy.

How does anyone know what they're thinking? How does anyone recognize the truth of what they're told?

Facts are like pomegranate seeds, packed in together and tenuously linked. Their weight accumulates, like stored energy, sometimes it blocks passage, tangles, and obstructs. Perception. Qualities of experience. Qualities of animal intuition.

Qualities of living with V. Lacking awareness of all natural things.

XXXV. EMERGENT RESPONSES

Harold's screen said:

Expect to witness odd occurrences in coming days: unexpected arrivals, black hole void-consuming energy, dark matter spilling. Crack numbers, calculate distances between stars, growing smaller. Dark matter seeps into head cloud, neuronal nebula.

How many ideas can anyone hold at one time? Too few, too few. His grasp growing, EMPATHY's working, but more worry. Hannah's absence wrapped around his body, constricted like moons spinning closer, boomeranging. People were off doing so many things simultaneously, it was hard to keep track of trying to imagine them all at once: gazing at screens, into lovers' eyes, fucking, staring into night sky, removing the heart from a body, holding it in hand, then slipping it into another, giving life. Sitting at work, shopping, awash in chemical currents, head against wall, capsules rolling down tongues, chemicals traveling through veins, a bright orange epiphany, pastel mellowing. Swallowing, sitting, memorizing.

Why had Hannah not come home? It was not too late, he knew. She could be functioning, without cracks, without having fallen. He could almost see her bright eyes.

PING

Suddenly, there it was. A red dot on the radius. On the north side, near the forest.

The opposite side of town. Real time. Jump! was his first impulse and he pulled on a shirt, backwards first, then right side out, stain on front, then traded it for a different one.

He opened the cupboard and from his organizer took two red capsules, placed them side by side on his tongue and washed them down, counted to three. Looked at the vial. Two more, he needed two more.

PING.

That's two.

How had he not realized his limits? Even simple calculus says fact acquisition could be graphed as a function of x. Eventually it will curve, slowing, approaching a limit. Perhaps his limits were smaller than most, or perhaps he'd pushed himself further. Or maybe none of this. So much within his mind was hidden. But clutter was now clearer. He'd found his way through. He would pay attention. He promised. His wager with the universe.

PING.

Coming closer, approaching the factory. A slow-moving curve. Was she walking? *Get into the car*, he thought, then he did. He entered the destination in the direction of her pings and pushed D=R=I=V=E.

ETA: 15 minutes. Car reversed into the street, drove past houses standing like immaculate boxes, some with walks and columns, others with porches, so many trimmed lawns. Then fields and warehouses and trailers and deserted lots. Then the rise of the hill, still ashy, but with new beams reaching toward the sky.

XXXVI. DISCONTINUATION OF USE

I put my chip in and turned on my device. *Within range*, it said. *Messages updating.* The notifications came one after another as if they'd been waiting:

IMAGE: Looters ransack stockpile storage site. Smoke rises above a string of doors at PRPL HILLS LIFE STORAGE. The sign emits a hazy light as bodies crawl through jammed doors.

IMAGE: City Hall protesters sit in the square, holding signs. "RELEASE SUPPLIES! Don't annihilate our children's minds!"

IMAGE: Clear capsules roll down conveyor belts, piles of powder accumulate, fall into larger piles, fill capsules, fill plastic bottles, glide through pneumatic tubes. Ticker tape says: *Production increases dramatically within a 500-mile radius.*

IMAGE: "And a new report this morning," the newscaster says, "the discovery of a possible disruption in the fabric of the universe."

IMAGE: A red Jeep dirt-caked, a front headlight

smashed. A woman stands in the distance, flanked b
officers. I barely make out her dark-rimmed eyes, h
puffy cheeks.

Was it Jai's jeep? Had to be? Front fender smashed
spread my fingers to enlarge the image. The face on
became wider and more distorted. What had happene
I wondered. And Celia—where was she?

WANTED it said across the bottom of the screen.

"Wanted," I said.

"They don't say wanted when they've been detaine
Azzie reminded.

"But wanted for what?"

"Looks like something to do with the factory fire."

"Wait—what!? I mean...there are so many red Jeep
There had been signs. Azzie had insinuated. But I hadr
taken her seriously. If that was the same Jeep, and if t
accusations were true, I didn't know what to make of
It couldn't be. Celia had to be free. I felt it in my bon
At least I wanted this to be true.

Behind us trees and fields and forest stretched. Ar
yet it was hard to believe that this too was real.

A beige sedan slowed on the side of the highway b
fore it stopped on the shoulder. I recognized this c
the shape of my father inside.

How did he find us?

I grabbed Azzie and pulled her behind a tree with n

The sedan's door opened, I saw a foot on the ground, then another.

"Hannah?" I heard Harold call. He looked hesitant at first, then got out. He was looking at his device and typing. He walked forward, then hoisted himself over the roadside barrier. Harold started wandering blindly into the woods toward us.

"Go!" Azzie said. She squeezed me then pushed me away.

I resisted and stood back with her. "But what do I say?"

Harold meeting us here was not something we'd anticipated. Though part of me rejoiced at seeing my father's large cheeks, his tuft of hair. To think, Harold had come to find me! He kept walking, and saying, *Hannah?* in a low groggy voice, as if he were asking a question of the world.

Azzie told me not to miss this chance. He was here.

She whispered, "We can't be seen together. Not here. Say you wandered to clear your head."

But we were together in this. That was our alibi, wasn't it? It didn't matter, I had to act. I decided I wouldn't say any more than I needed to. Harold was getting closer.

I stepped out and walked away quickly to make sure Azzie was out of sight.

I walked toward him for a bit before I called out, "Harold?"

He jumped, like he hadn't expected me.

"Hannah!" he said. I ran toward him and he pulled me to his belly. "I've been so worried. Where have you been?"

I couldn't tell him. I lifted my head up and he was looking down at me.

His eyes looked so sad.

I turned and looked in the back seat.

Empty.

"I needed time..."

"...I know, I know, your mother.... Judy panicky, you don't have to explain."

"Well yes but..."

"But what I'm saying is. I'm saying. You're here. There's time.... I'm glad you're ... found. Just get in the car?"

Image as if acquisition. Of fact, of knowledge, of possession.
A screen as passage.
Imperative distance.

XXXVII.

Nothing was quite the same again, and not in ways I would've anticipated. Harold and I came home to an empty house that afternoon and sat on the couch as he cued the projection of northern lights. He closed the curtains, and I crawled under his arm. Esmerelda came and sat on my lap, and Ismelda nuzzled up against my side, as we watched the astral blues and greens move across the dark night of the screen. After a while Harold asked me what had happened, where had I gone?

I didn't know what to say. I couldn't betray our whereabouts of the past two days, that we'd crossed the perimeter and gone deep into the trees. I knew he didn't expect an explanation per se, but he was worried in a way I'd never seen. He looked like he'd been shaken awake. When I'd seen his red, watery eyes my first thought was the toxicities, but he said he'd been taking medication for a *condition*.

Empathy, had I heard of it?

I nodded yes. I told him, *recently*. I had feelings, and feelings about his feelings, and I wanted to push them away. It all felt so overwrought. But also, I felt a deep longing. I asked him, how long had he been taking it?

He said he didn't know. A while at least. He only now realized he was feeling its effects, this rush of loneliness. My absence and the catastrophe at the factory, the backorders and anxiety. He said this was the worst feeling, and he wondered why he continued taking it knowing Empathy was enabling this ability. Until now. Now he knew without a doubt.

I noticed he spoke with fewer gaps, fewer *hmmms*, fewer awkward pauses that just dropped off. I tried to imagine the ways he'd have been without this condition. But also, I couldn't imagine Harold any other way. I loved him but I resented the factory.

Dad, I said, while huddled there in the dark. I never called him that. I told him I didn't want to take enhancements, didn't want anything to do with the factory, their R&D program, whatever it might offer me. I told him that I'd hate my life.

Harold said that hating my life was a very serious thing. But also I was just shy of seventeen, and how could I understand the consequences of my decisions? He suggested I let it sit. And so we sat together in silence.

Azzie messaged me not long after. "Made it back," she texted. She asked about the *Harold situation*. I told her not to worry, that he suspected nothing and I hadn't had to say anything yet. She said that Trinie was at the hospital, working another double. Beds were filled though the toxic effects were easing and recoveries were hastening.

get this, Azzie messaged, *T was home, left a note.* Trinie was worried when we weren't there, not answering her messages, which was not a way Azzie was with her, like ever.

u think she knws? I responded, to which she replied, ¯_(ツ)_/¯

Trinie had reason to be suspicious. But also, she'd been working a string of sixteen-hour days so didn't have the time to uncover our lies. I told Azzie we should meet up later, the next day, whenever, but IRL. I wanted to say nothing more until then.

Judy was warm enough when she arrived home later that evening. She'd had a series of meetings, she explained, something to do with what she called "activating stockpiles." I didn't question that this was important but I wondered why she hadn't tried to come earlier when she'd heard I was home. She hugged me and kissed me, said she'd been so worried in the high, fraught voice that she used when she didn't want to reveal how angry she was. "You gave us such a fright." She said Azzie had been in touch with her on my behalf, but why hadn't I just answered her calls?

"Have you talked to Billy?" I asked.

"Of course I have. We've been working around the clock together."

"He told you about the Azpire? What a fucking

name."

She nodded yes, "Have you been taking?" She didn't wait for me to answer. "Never mind, we'll start tonight."

"That's not possible. I'm not taking it. I'm done with V., Azpire, whatever."

"But Hannah. People are waiting hours for a dose, for even a chance at one."

"You'll have to force it down my throat."

"You can't be serious," is all she said. She looked over her shoulder to Harold and said, "Har, back me up, dear."

His shoulders were tense like a freaked-out kid. "Perhaps we let the dust settle? Let's pick it up tomorrow?"

She said she couldn't understand why I kept thwarting myself. "It's not your decision, Hannah. You may think you know better but..." She had fire in her eyes. She directed Harold to bring the box beside her bag forward. He did as she requested. She opened the box and ran her hand over the packaging.

An entire case of V., all for me. Of course she'd had access. I laughed.

"It's not funny. *NOT funny*," she repeated.

"Okay, okay."

"I've risked so much and this is the thanks I get."

"And I thank you."

"Your sarcasm is insulting."

"No I mean, I am glad you're concerned but, I wish you'd listen."

"Listen to what?!"

I looked over at Harold. I wished he'd play more of an intermediary. Whenever Judy was around he was cowed. Why did he never advocate for me?

Judy and I stood in silent opposition. We could've stood there all night.

"Fine," she said with surrender. "Your father is right. We could all use some sleep."

We didn't have it out that night, but I knew it wasn't over. Judy was on my mind as I tried to fall asleep. I loved my mother if love was a tether. I wondered how I could so resent someone whose body I emerged from. She'd had similar feelings toward her own mother for her own reasons (*too slothful, not on top of things, disengaged, among her litanies*). Now her antipathy was directed toward me. I know the blame wasn't all with me or all with her but lay between us somehow in how we related. Perhaps *blame* wasn't the right word. Maybe it was the resentment that she'd spent her life combating with aplomb that I'm inheriting. I wondered, was I the harbinger of animosity, or articulating the distrust she directed toward me first? Fucked if I knew.

Judy and I passed most of the next morning in a standoff that picked up where we'd left off. I refused the VALEDICTORIAN though I'd appeased her by taking other enhancements. Once she left for her afternoon appointments, I slept, and I slept like I hadn't slept in months, at least in my own bed.

Azzie came by in the evening and we went out to the back deck. Our faces covered, we spoke in whispers. The air still smelled like burnt toast and Factory Hill was dark. Azzie said Trinie was at the hospital again. She'd worked seven days straight already. Azzie looked concerned, maybe even like she'd been crying.

"You're not looking so good. Did Trinie buy our cover?" I asked.

She shrugged. "Not really. She isn't letting up. First thing she asked was where we'd been. She knew I was supposed to be watching after you. I told her we'd gone to Jeni's."

Trinie had asked if she knew anything about Celia's whereabouts. Azzie said she'd feigned ignorance but felt panicky. She didn't lie well to her mother. Trinie knew this too, probably better than anyone. Trinie said there was no video footage of Celia escaping the ward, no witnesses, and to disappear like that raised suspicions. Likely had required outside help. She had asked Azzie again if she knew anything more or had any ideas of where Celia had gone. Said it was dangerous for Celia to not have the support she was receiving at the hospital.

"Do you think she suspects us? What did you say?"

"Oh, you know something like, *Fuck no, of course not.* I told her that we'd gone over to Jeni's and I was so anxious the only thing that calmed me down was cumming and so we stayed up all night fucking. And that I'd slept all the next day."

"You think she bought that."

"I dunno. All I have to do is talk about fucking and she clams up. I'm just worried she's not the only one we'll need to convince. She said a psych nurse ghosted. Didn't show up for her shift the night of the fire or since."

"You think it was Jai?"

"Doubt it? I thought Jai only worked weekends. I know Trinie won't say anything about us. I just don't want her to get blamed. She brought us to visit her on the ward, you know."

"But that was different."

"Not really."

I could tell Azzie didn't like having to create so many lies to cover up a larger one. She was still worried about Celia, she said.

I was too. But there wasn't anything we could undo. She'd been determined to go out there with or without us. I asked if she'd told Jeni she was our cover.

"In not so many words. I mean, I'm heading to her house after this and will make sure."

She could see my face turning.

"Look, I'm not going to say a word about where

we've been."

"Okay." What else could I say?

"What about Judy?"

"Just the usual."

"Good."

She opened her banana pill box with a twist and tapped a small pink tablet in her hand offering it to me.

"Nah, I'm good."

She looked disappointed.

"Just, not tonight," I said.

She implored me with her sad eyes.

"Keep me posted, okay?" I said as I hugged her.

To have been offline in the days after Lumena burned and to return to see the detritus really messed with my head. I felt like I needed a reboot. The flames proliferated on replay, the count of how many were suffering chemical burns, the heaves and what have you only increased. Classes were moved online completely. No one knew how long this would last. We were to filter our air, ration our meds, boil our water, until the atmosphere cleared.

It didn't help that we didn't talk about any of this at home. The effects, the madness in my head, my visions of chimps, the reality that my mind was going in and out. Or about what was happening in Lumena: why parents were protesting, why people were blaming environmentalists for meddling. That others were panicking and rationing and just pressing *buy buy buy* to accumulate as many supplements as they could as if an excess of everything would keep them safe. I would've asked why they needed to feel like fucking kingpins just to ride out the chaos.

Azzie texted again the next morning to say she had allayed Trinie's concerns. But there were more headlines, she said, and that worried her. She then sent a series of links. The first was about a group of environmentalists wanted for questioning, who were seen monitoring the aftereffects of the fire. The details about their role or what questions the authorities wanted to pose were murky to say the least. There was a photo and a list of names I didn't recognize—though two women in the photo were dead ringers for Jules and Jai. One hadn't been seen since the beginning of the month, and the other had been spotted on factory grounds in the days following the fire. She was said to be wanted for questioning for fearmongering, for monitoring without permits and for trespassing on factory grounds.

Another link detailed how Celia was now registered as a missing person. Her parents were offering a reward for information leading to her return. Celia was last seen taking her afternoon meds, accepting her dinner, and then taking a rest before the night nurse checked in to find an empty bed. Or so the

article said. Celia's exit hadn't been caught on surveillance cameras. She hadn't been spotted by anyone
on her way out. *An inside job*, they speculated. *An ab-
duction*, even. Celia's parents seemed to care more for
her now as they spoke about missing their daughter,
what a bright soul she possessed (*her mother's words*);
they said she'd given them so much joy despite her
troubles, for which she'd been getting help.

All I could think was, *you hypocrites.*

When I got up the nerve to walk downstairs, I found
Judy had left already. The house was empty. I felt
relief knowing we wouldn't have another standoff.
In the kitchen I found a cup of supplements on the
counter, as well as a note:

*full day of meetings, emergency still in effect, distribu-
tion and fires to put out—ha! I'm sure you'll be happier
on your own, but please, Hannah, I implore you, for my
sake and yours, take the pills I've left.*

I looked at the cup filled with squares and suns
and bright colored capsules. I wanted only the ra-
diance of their hues. I started opening cabinets and
drawers in search of that box Judy had prostrated. It
wasn't in the cabinet or under the sink, and it wasn't
beside the vials on the counter. I looked in the pantry,
in the storage closet, in her home office, and then in

her bedroom, and the master bath. I found it in the closet, on the top shelf. A corner of the box poked out from behind a stack of towels. She had known I'd come looking.

I paused. I didn't feel guilty per se, but I knew I was crossing another boundary. I perched on the counter so I could reach the box and take it down. I placed it on the bathroom counter and considered my options. I could flush them all down the toilet. But, no, I knew what I'd do with it. I placed my cup of pills in the box, closed the top, and stuffed it into my pack.

I threw on some clothes, covered my face with a scarf, and walked down to Factory Hill where a crowd had gathered. They'd been there every day since the fire, I'd heard. All faces were covered, each of us was encapsulated in our own way, and yet the energy was mounting. It felt like something was happening but what it was I couldn't quite say.

There was a group of mothers who talked about baselines to anyone who passed by. They worried they wouldn't have access to V. to maintain this for their children, not to mention themselves. And even then, who would get what and when?

Others carried signs that said:

> RELEASE SUPPLIES!
> IT'S OUR CHILDREN'S MINDS!
> LAY BARE LUMENA'S LIES!

I walked among them and that's where I met a man streaming video footage of Ms. Tigue, though a gaunt ghost of her former self. She was in bed, wearing a purple velour house dress. I asked how he knew her, and how she was doing, and he said he was Sara Tigue's cousin.

I said it was horrible what had happened to her, and that I had been a witness. I was relieved she wasn't dead. He said she was still recovering. I asked him if she'd been trying to send us a message.

Not sure what she'd have been trying to say. She surely didn't intend to induce her state. He said her parents were tube feeding her. He said that he'd felt helpless to do anything to intervene and he'd started obsessively searching for and reading more about V.'s side effects and interactions, and for other supplements too. *She's not the only one.*

I told him I wanted to hear everything he knew.

He said that would take too long, but he could tell me some things. If I wanted to give him my contact info he'd forward more.

I said yes, of course.

He said things that echoed what the nurse had told me. That Lumena curates the studies they release, to make their supplements look more advantageous. They downplay adverse reactions and mental fragility caused by a multitude of supplements, most notably VALEDICTORIAN. Like they won't acknowledge V.'s role in Cognitive Drift even though the correlation has been firmly established.

I nodded and said I'd just heard similar things. That all of this was not new to me. Dr Billy had always claimed our not having access to V. is far worse for humanity.

The man said he'd spent time connecting the pieces he'd found and was trying to make sense of them. But the pieces could be connected in a multiplicity of ways. He told me not to take his word for it, "Hearsay is close to heresy, they say."

I said, "No, I believe you." I said I was there when Tigue had OD'd, and how odd that now we'd meet. I said the memories kept coming back despite my Cognitive Release.

This exchange reminded me of a line from Percy Shelley's essay on atheism that had struck me when I first read it when researching for Crawford's class.

Truth has always been found to promote the best interests of mankind.

Somehow this had been so controversial that the essay had gotten him expelled from university. His words continue to stay with me, especially now.

I kept wandering and drifting though this drifting was different. I'd never witnessed people talking openly about anger and the ways the factory saw value only in perpetuating their profits and a cycle of dependence.

I was told that Lumena engaged in animal testing. I was shocked. There was a primate lab not terribly far away but forever away in the sense of its location far beyond Lumena Hills. Even worse, the lab had left animals no longer of use to fend for themselves on an island floating in the middle of some lake. I made note to myself that I needed to learn more about this island and these chimps. It was preposterous, really. Someone said they'd been left for dead and would've perished if it hadn't been for some environmentalists who'd stepped in and had started feeding and tending to them. No one knew of a chimp-cam set up on the island, though they seemed to think it was possible. I mean, it likely wasn't. The landscape had looked almost tropical. But at this moment anything felt possible.

I walked in a stupor, just trying to process my sense of a world caving in while it seemed another was opening.

I came to a line of tents set up as a series of relief stations. Behind them I found folding tables stacked with goods: bottles of e-lyte+ water and packets of Liquid EnerG and HiKal and vials full of assorted supplements.

I took off my pack, placed it on the table, withdrew Judy's box and set it beside a case of used H2O bottles. So many people wanted this box's contents, needed it even. Desperately. I didn't want to discard it during a crisis. Make matters worse. But I didn't want to be tied to it or its contents. I didn't want to have Judy implicated, either, even though I had considered this.

I stood there for a moment. I took a sip of my e-lyte+ water, gave the box my benediction, and walked away. I felt light, exhilarated even.

When I went home that evening, Judy asked me what I'd done with "it."

I said I didn't know what she was talking about.

She said, "I'm not stupid, Hannah."

I said, "Ok, yes. I took it with me today."

"And now?" She glared.

I shrugged. Mumbled something about giving them away.

Judy got all red in the face. She reached for a portrait I'd made of her and threw it across the room. It hit the sink and shattered into pieces. She paused and sipped from her water with tense lips. Said nothing still as she walked up the stairs, pounding them with her feet, then slammed the bedroom door. She wouldn't come out when I begged her to talk to me, to at least listen to my reasoning.

When I told Azzie about what went down and my leaving a box of VALEDICTORIAN outside a relief tent, she was like, "Are you crazy?" She demanded to know why I hadn't offered it to her first. I said the thought hadn't occurred to me. She seemed hurt in a way I'd never seen.

"I would've done it for you."

"You know I wouldn't have wanted it."

"Come on. I mean if the situation were reversed."

I didn't have a good answer. I said I'd secretly hoped she'd want to stop too. Knowing all the dangers and all.

She said I was being petulant—I hated that word—that throwing away that box of V. was just a big fuck-you to Judy. And why did I always have to be so obvi? Her anger was starting to feel like darts thrown.

"I'm just so sick of it. All of it," I said. I just wanted to make sure that the box was irretrievable. How could Azzie not understand why I did this?

She did and she didn't.

Judy didn't disown me exactly, but life under the same roof was tense. Azzie offered an open invitation to stay with her despite her frustration. I took her up on this but it posed its own complications. Like I was always in the way, crashing on either the large roll-out mattress in the corner or pulling out the living room couch. It was fine for a night or two but it didn't take long to feel my welcome wearing.

Azzie kept taking—V., supplements, all of it. I hadn't expected her to stop just because I did, but I wished she did. We'd been comrades. I wanted her to tell me that we'd done the right thing, that together we'd find a way to fight the system. But Azzie worried we'd really fucked up: like what if Trinie lost her job because of us. She didn't want to mess with her education, to be stuck working night shifts and run ragged when she was old enough to have kids. She said that if we were found out there would be consequences.

I wasn't planning to be found out, I'd told her.

I was just doing what I had to do.

It still breaks me to think of the way Azzie distanced herself from me when I started going to the demonstrations. She wouldn't come even when I asked her to just come, walk with me, and see. She always had something else to do, somewhere else to be. And then she went back to school.

She didn't want to meet the contact Jules had given us either. Said it wasn't worth the risk of betraying Celia's confidences but she wasn't going to stop me.

I don't think she thought I'd go alone, but I got Jeni to give me a ride out to the far east side, not far from where we'd gone to the rooftop party. Margo lived in a high rise, in #16B. I rang up from downstairs and when she answered she buzzed me in. Margo cracked the door, at first all I could see were her pale eyes and her long charcoal hair hanging over them. She asked the reason for my calling. I mentioned Jules. She paused, messed with some material in her hands, opened the door wider and motioned for me to come in. She said she was on a deadline and didn't have much time. I was struck by the large windows that let in great amounts of light. Two rooms were filled with linens and banners, with bureaus and myriad organizers containing threads and yarns, thimbles and needles, materials strewn from one side of the room to another. Margo said she wasn't sure she could help me but she'd teach me to sew if I wanted to learn. It was an informal offer and soon I started coming, and often staying late. She had multiple sewing machines but much of the intricate work she did by hand. I learned from Margo. I started sewing by hand, slow-stitch, drawing lines and curves with pencil onto linens, cutting patterns, and watching Margo piece it all together as she explained her processes.

Soon Margo's sewing room became my sleeping

place more nights than not. I slept on the daybed, never lacked for linen, and always woke with the sun. There was space and a sense that I could breathe in this place. Margo said she liked me, and I was earning my keep, not that I had to—she knew what I was going through—and handed me a set of keys. She said she'd make room in the corner for some of my possessions, so it could feel cozier. I think she took pity on me. There's no explanation for her kindness, for her taking me in. I mean, even when my own mother wouldn't talk to me. I returned home to see Harold but I felt the resentment and hostilities lingering as if the house held her emotions too—

The last time I went when I knew the house was empty. I took an extra-large duffel bag from the basement, packed my clothes, my favorite portraits, including ones of Celia and Azzie, and a jar of moon rocks Harold had given me. I sat with Ismelda and Esmerelda for a long time, just nuzzling them and giving them treats. I wished I could take them with me, but I knew I could barely take care of myself. They were better off here for the time being. I packed the few lists I'd printed and images and my materials related to the endangered species, and items leftover from our ceremonies. I packed my gloves and thought how I missed using them, and Azzie's face. Now that I had them again, I thought I'd begin a new series documenting faces of the people gathering at Factory

Hill's base.

Harold was upset when he discovered I'd cleaned out my things, but he still messaged me. He sent money every so often and cheesy video clips and said that he missed me. Eventually he asked if he could come visit me at Margo's. Judy didn't want him to, he said. She wanted him to pressure me into coming home and apologizing.

The first time he came to Margo's he admired the windows and the weather balloons she'd made that now hung from the ceiling. I asked him to sit for a portrait. He told me to wait. He had something for me. I said no, no, he had this look I wanted to capture. Somehow his face was more alive. It had a different feeling. When I ran my hands over his eyes and thick cheeks, his colors were brighter, shades of green, orange and yellow running together. There was a shape to his face, and when done it looked almost ecstatic? Yes, at least in comparison to its heaviness before, that almost resembled a lump of clay. Harold seemed satisfied that I was fed and cared for in some way. As he left, he slipped me a package he'd kept in his coat. I placed the box on the table and left it there for a while, dreading to think of what it might contain. I waited until I finished processing Harold's portrait, until I had heated some grains to eat. I opened the box. Inside I found Harold's favorite pair of binoculars.

XXXVIII.

Three semesters later, I stood on the rooftop of Margo's building. I was absent from the graduation ceremony taking place that morning but I had a birds-eye view atop this high rise at the edge of town. I could see the stadium in the distance, the seats in the field that held my former classmates. Surely Crawford and Dr. Billy and Judy were there, as was Azzie. I'd heard she'd done very well. Salutatorian. I'd heard that Celia's mother was going to sit in Celia's seat and that she'd be given an honorary degree. No traces had ever been found.

I imagined my former classmates in miniature, wearing their silver caps and purple robes as they glided across the stage and were congratulated and handed fake diplomas that would be replaced once all the ceremoniousness had concluded. And where were they off to? To other factory towns, to the learning centers funded with grants for science and tech, to labs and rooms walled in pixelation. To research labs where they injected newfangled chemicals into animals for testing, to design studios focused on marketing, to call centers and warehouses storing raw materials.

From where I stood they were so small, they

almost looked like little pills rolling across a conveyor belt, gathering until they flipped their caps in a shower of silver and purple confetti.

The shortage of Valedictorian was a blip in Lumena's history. As soon as the supply lines opened—and it wasn't long—the factory put people to work again. Of the protestors who were left, many became discouraged and drifted away. I formed many more questions but found few answers.

We formed a small steady group that met regularly. We were the curious eccentrics, the unemployed and unemployable, those who were shut out in some way. We each had our own starting point but agreed on the need for dialogue and transparency. Not all stayed on. It was okay. I didn't plan to spend the rest of my days here either.

From this roof, I had also watched as shipments began to arrive on trucks and trailers in twos and threes, crossing the bridge at the bottom of the hill, circling up and slowing, leaning in with each curve. The trucks unloaded on a dock that faced the forest. The sun set on this side and fell into a deep awful redness just as the trucks purged their loads of boxes and powders and concrete and beams. The trucks were then loaded again later in the evening before they barreled down the road.

My devices kept streaming messages sponsored by Lumena, about community, about uniting, about chemical maintenance as a necessity. About *progress*. But what was a community built upon dependence? I'd seen images of miracle powders in pinks and greens and yellows, piled high, filling tanks, and beakers and cylinders. So many small particles, so much sunset, so much dust.

I hadn't heard from Celia, not in all this time. There'd been no word since we left her with Jai—no paper trail, no traces. No alternative, I assumed. But I couldn't know for sure. Whatever I'd seen of that red Jeep on the news that night had been inconsequential. I learned Jules had been taken in for questioning but there was nothing else in the public record. I couldn't find anything more about it in my feeds no matter how long I searched, and this had nothing to do with the intermittent periods of cotton-headedness I sometimes still experienced.

I didn't search too deeply. I didn't know who might be monitoring me. Still, I wished I would hear from Celia, just a note with no return address that said something like:

loves! we're in Guatemala or Panama or Guadalajara or Chile or Antarctica, I can't tell you! maybe all and none. just a quick note to tell you I'm safe, my mind has gained strength and this adventure exceeds what I'd imagined. We've been talking of a trip back your way, you'll be the first to know when we do.

'til then don't worry about me.
sending love and fishes.
full-stop.
xoxoxo
C

Sometimes I dreamt of Celia flying above the rocky cliffs on the Sea of Cortez, dipping down with her mouth open, scooping up fish like she was a pelican, then joining Jai, on the ridge, perched in the sun. The fish replicate, one jumping from the mouth of another as they slip back into the sea.

Without classes, without V., without a focus on accumulating, I had so much time. It stretched so wide and I filled it with so many things, like sunbathing on the roof, walking deep into the woods in attempts to teach myself foraging, and protesting at the base of the hill. Often I was the only one greeting the procession of employees on their way to their first shift, before they crossed the bridge and were ferried up to the factory.

With Margo in the afternoons, I had been making sails and weather balloons, kites and windsocks constructed from all kinds of weatherproof materials. She encouraged me to start making my own balloons and aided me when I was overcome by their formidable size. We started staging interventions—we painted messages in electric greens and purples like

UNFILTERED
EMBRACE ENNUI
LOVE'S A BOMB

These messages had to be written large enough to be seen from the ground. We would inflate the balloons on the roof of her building and let them float off. Sometimes we would mount them on the roof so that the messages would hover over us. It was a larger undertaking than it sounds.

This is what we were doing as I watched the graduation ceremony, sending a message I had derived:

? YR ANSWER

A simple statement that I hoped would plant a seed in other minds. And yet I had no expectations.

I've learned so much in this time, so much more than I'd ever learned in the classroom, from a chemical, from a screen. I try not to become discouraged by the doors that have shut, the ways I've been shunned, especially by my mother who I still haven't seen. Azzie has come to visit me, only a handful of times. Now she barely acknowledges me if we pass on the street. There's almost an unbearable weight to our greeting.

I'd never thought I'd feel so futile and filled with wonder simultaneously.

And still. I know we are all connected through the energy of electrons firing. We are connected through the air we breathe. This air is strong enough to hold an airplane. This air is expansive enough to allow for so much information. This air is filled with so much passing through, the particles, the electrons and protons and neutrons and neutrinos and the god particle too. Information is passing, moving through us, and yet how much is passing us by?

It's dizzying to consider the information penetrating our orifices all of the time. Information spreading like electricity, divining, traveling through this vast ocean of air.

We are absorbing in excess, as in, at capacity.

We are saturated.

The other thing about this day? I received a message. I had been waiting. Soon I will be on my way to be introduced to the chimps, to feed and care for them, and to learn more about the ways this is done. To learn more about how they were abandoned by Lumena and the others who stepped in. I am looking forward to meeting the chimps. I mean, it's hard to not feel like I might recognize them. I know now that they aren't the same chimps I'd watched so devotedly on my screens. But even so, nothing will compare to meeting them.

I think I could make a life of this? But also, it's just a beginning. For now there's no other place: Only here. Only between. I am so small in this town in this world in this universe, and yet I can't shake the sense of its immensity.

ACKNOWLEDGMENTS

A million thank you's wouldn't suffice for Amanda Goldblatt's vision, labor, and support of this book. Her belief in this manuscript and ability to see its possibilities have been essential to its becoming. Thank you to Rebecca Elliott, for their friendship, collaboration, and their tireless and wonderful work on this book and so many others. To Suzanne Gold who ran with inspiration. To Molly Gunther for her exceptional word savviness. To the wisdom and generosity of early readers Patrick Cottrell, Megan Kaminski, Susan Chi, David Rogers, Suzanne Scanlon, Rita Bullwinkel, Sam Ramos, Megan Burbank, Rebekah Hall, and Heather McShane. To Marcy Rae Henry who has assiduously commented on the first half but has yet to read the end. To Poppy Brandes and to Miranda Steffens for our walks and conversations. To Kamilah Foreman and Sarah Dodson for publishing an excerpt in *MAKE*. To Olena Jennings for reading and for publishing an excerpt in *KGB Bar Lit*. To Jen Karmin for Roger Dodger residency time and so much else. To John Wilmes, for agreeing.

To Samantha Hunt, Patrick Cottrell, and Sarah Gerard, whose minds and words dazzle me. I'm so grateful for your support and for your kind words about this book.

To Lynne Tillman whose work has been a lodestar and whose friendship has meant everything. To Diane Williams whose class at the Mercantile Library was a revelation. To Betsy VanOot and Tom Gazzola, early teachers who made more of a difference than they knew. To Beth Nugent who read every messy early draft and whose conversations about writing and process were so vital. To wisdom and play imbibed during grad school workshops with Sara Levine and Jesse Ball. To the writers from Stephen Wright's 92nd Street Y workshop many years ago who read drafts of a first failed attempt at a novel and helped me persevere. To Cathy Siebold, Michele Gaspar, and Jeremy Bloomfield, without whose support this book would not be.

To Christopher Byrd for our impassioned attempt at making blissed out fucking dreams reality. To Erin Schiesel, Heather Hurford, Erika Biddle-Stavrakos, Sunitha Vege, Misty Donaldson, Caron Levis, and Chris LaRochelle. To my brother Stephen, my first creative collaborator. To my Aunt Jean for so many things, not the least of which has been providing nook to write in while gazing at the sea. To my parents, who gave me a love of books and stories. To K&B. And never least, to David, ever my harbor.

Anne K. Yoder's fiction, essays, and criticism have appeared in *Fence*, *BOMB*, *Tin House*, *NY Tyrant*, and *MAKE*, among other publications. She writes, lives, and occasionally dispenses pharmaceuticals in Chicago.